BEHIND THE BRIGHT LIGHTS AND GLITTERING STARS OF GOLDEN-AGE HOLLYWOOD...

"ELIZABETH CROSS." SHE SHOOK his hand briefly, but when she tried to let go, he pulled her a little closer. Simon instinctively started toward them, but a warning hand from Grant kept him from intervening.

"You are," Thorn said, seeming to look for the word in her eyes, "lovely. So...pure."

Thorn regarded Simon for a brief moment, a flash of a smile touching his eyes as their gazes met. Thorn might have been speaking to Elizabeth but it was really Simon he was talking to. It was a strange feeling, but Simon was sure of that. Just as he was sure this man was dangerous. He couldn't put his finger on what it was, but every instinct in his body was warning him that something was wrong. Something was very wrong...

...LURKS AN INSIDIOUS DARKNESS.

PRAISE FOR THE DEVIL'S DUE

"There are many fans of films from Hollywood's golden age in the 1930's. I am not one of them. Having said that, I found Martin's tale set in the glamor of old Hollywood as irresistible as a seven-layer chocolate cake smothered in rich ganache. May I have another slice, please?"
- Cidney Swanson, author of the *Rippler* Trilogy

"Monique Martin just keeps getting better. In the fourth book of Martin's time travel mystery series, Elizabeth and Simon, joined by the incomparable Jack Wells, face their most chillling foe yet. Part sexy romp through old Hollywood glamour, part heartfelt tale of loss and regret, The Devil's Due will capture readers with its clever twists, lush descriptions, and witty dialogue."
- Melissa F. Miller, author of the *Sasha McCandless* Series

"The Devil's Due is the next great installment in what has become one of my all time favorite series'. Monique Martin's ability to transport the reader to different places and times is so complete that I find myself able to close my eyes months later and still picture the setting as though I'd actually been there."
- J.M. Pierce, author of *The Shadow* Series.

"It's worth reading just for the description of a movie studio lot in the golden age of Hollywood. But sexy Simon, a gorgeous love story, and a couple of fascinating twists will keep you turning the pages - and eagerly awaiting the next book in the series."
- Debora Geary, author of *A Modern Witch* Series

MONIQUE MARTIN

The Devil's Due

Out of Time Series
Book 4

Cover Photo: Karen Wunderman
Cover Layout & Interior Formatting: TERyvisions

ISBN 10: 0984660755
ISBN 13: 978-0-9846607-5-9

For more information, please contact
writtenbymonique@gmail.com
Or visit: www.moniquemartin.weebly.com

Acknowledgements

THIS BOOK WOULD NOT have been possible without the help and support of many people: Robin, who keeps me from going insane, guides me and makes me laugh; Dad and Anne; Mom and George; Eddie and Carole; Michael; Melissa; Cindy; JM; Deb, and all the wonderful people who sent notes of encouragement along the way.

I'd also like to thank the thousands of people who help preserve the past through books, websites, museums and sheer will.

The Out of Time Series
by Monique Martin

Out of Time

When the Walls Fell

Fragments

The Devil's Due

Please check Monique's website,
http://moniquemartin.weebly.com/
for news of new and upcoming books!

THE DEVIL'S DUE

Out of Time, Book 4

Monique Martin

PROLOGUE

1933—LOS ANGELES, CALIFORNIA

THEY ALWAYS RAN—FROM THE man, from themselves, from the inevitable.

Daniel hated this place. Everything about it was a lie, from the promises of work to the endless sunshine. He knew there was no escape, but even in his despair he wanted to live. His feet slipped out from under him as he slid across the gravel of the Cornfield Yard. Even the name was another lie. There was no corn here. There probably never had been.

In the distance, somewhere in the night, he heard the rumble of an engine getting closer, wheels turning, racing just as he was, on a track and no way to get off. Daniel grabbed the edge of one of the parked, empty boxcars and yanked himself to a stop. He reached for the lever to the door and thought about trying to hide inside, but he knew, if he stopped, it would be the last thing he did.

He pushed off again. His new boots struggled to find traction in the loose gravel. He ran between the long lines of rail cars, sleeping giants, cold and dark. Until a week ago, he'd thought it had all been a dream. But then the man had come to remind him. His time was almost up.

It had been a moment of weakness, of desperation, and it would be the end of him. He knew that. His legs burned from the effort to escape his fate. He ran between the huge iron snakes with only the moon watching. But, he knew he wasn't alone. The man was here. Somewhere. Waiting.

As soon as the thought entered his mind, he felt it. The hairs on the back of his neck prickled. The whistle from an approaching train cut through the quiet. Daniel spun around. Not more than twenty feet away, the tall, dark silhouette of the man stood on the empty tracks. He waited, patient and still.

Panic and sooty air clogged Daniel's throat. He turned, jumped between stationary cars, nearly tripping over their coupling before popping out on the other side. He ran as fast as his feet could carry him—between cars, under them, through them. He ran.

The distant train whistle blared again, louder, closer. Daniel skidded to a stop. He drew two quick terrified breaths before running again. He ran down the length of the Southern Pacific counting the cars, just as he'd always done as a boy. 23, 24, 25…

He felt the rumble of the coming train behind him. 26, 27, 28…If he could just make it to the end, he might be free. 29, 30, 31!

He clutched the handrail of the last car and swung himself around the end of the parked train. He leapt across the tracks, then across another set. The third would be his last. The headlight from the engine flashed brightly as though it were as surprised as he was. Even at the slow yard speed, the train was too close and moving too fast. Daniel barely had time to close his eyes. And then it was over.

The train rolled past, car after car, until finally the last of it disappeared into the night. The wind from the passing train briefly blew open the dark man's coat. He pulled down his hat and waited.

A small, brown mottled butterfly rested on the back of Daniel's tattered and bloody coat. It spread its wings and nervously took flight. The man pulled a handkerchief from his pocket and used it to capture the butterfly from the air. He held it gently in his hand. The butterfly fluttered inside the handkerchief, pushing against the fabric in a panic. The man watched it impassively for a moment, before stuffing it into his pocket.

Without even so much as a glance at Daniel's body, he turned and walked away.

CHAPTER ONE

PRESENT DAY—SANTA BARBARA, CALIFORNIA

IT WAS A PERFECT day. It wasn't because the sun was bright and warm or that the ocean sent a cool breeze over the hill at Elings Park, or even that the roses on the arched pergola behind him all seemed to bloom today. It was because of her.

Simon barely heard the birds in the trees or the rustle of the leaves. He barely noticed the man they'd hired to perform the ceremony or Jack Wells as he tugged repeatedly and nervously on his collar. All Simon could think of was Elizabeth, the woman who would soon be his wife.

He liked the sound of that word. Wife. He'd tried it on many times in the months before he'd worked up the courage to propose and each time it felt right. For nearly all of his life, Simon had accepted that a family wasn't in his future. His own family had soured the taste of it and his solitary life had all but ensured it. Then Elizabeth came along and everything changed.

Dear God, he'd been so terrified those first few weeks. Falling in love with her put him in a near constant state of fear, fear of loving her, fear of losing her. When he'd finally come to accept that, despite the absurdity of it all, she loved him as much as he loved her, the world seemed to start again. And now, here he was, waiting to make her his wife.

Simon stared down toward the small copse of trees and his breath caught in his throat as she stepped forward. She was so beautiful it made his heart swell and ache. They'd decided on a private ceremony and now he was gladder of it than ever. He didn't want to share her or this moment with anyone else.

Jack and the Justice of the Peace were there by necessity, but he willed them away in his mind, until it was just Elizabeth and he. Step by step, she walked toward him. Alone. That had been his one regret. Her father had long passed and anyone else who could have served was lost in time long past. She was alone. But after today neither of them would be alone again.

Elizabeth caught his eye and smiled as though she'd read his mind. She had a way of doing that, a way of seeing inside him, of somehow seeing things in him he could not see himself. Simon smiled back hoping he could be the man she saw in her heart.

She took a last few steps and came to his side. She shifted the small bouquet of flowers she'd picked that morning into her left hand and Simon took hold of her right.

They both turned to face the Justice of the Peace who smiled at them before beginning. "Marriage is a promise, made in the hearts of two people who love each other, which takes a lifetime to fulfill. Within the circle of its love, marriage encompasses all of life's most important relationships. A wife and a husband are each other's teacher, listener, critic, partner and best friend. It is into this state that Elizabeth and Simon wish to enter."

The Justice nodded to Simon indicating it was his time to speak his vows. Simon had written a dozen versions and thrown them all away. In the end, he'd decided to trust his heart and let it speak.

Simon gazed down at their joined hands. He gently rubbed his thumb back and forth across the soft skin of the back of her hand before trusting his voice enough to speak. He looked up unto her eyes and, as always, found what he needed there. "When I first met you, you were irritating."

Elizabeth laughed. "I'd grown so used to being alone," he continued. "I'd gone from accepting to embracing my misery. And then there was you. And no matter how hard I resisted, how painfully hard I resisted loving you, there was no escape and I thank whatever powers might be every day for that."

A tear slipped down Elizabeth's cheek and Simon brushed it away. His heart was so full it ached in his chest. "My dear Miss West, there is not a day that has come before or a day that has yet to be that I want to spend with anyone but you. I love you more with every passing second, with every beat of my heart. There is nothing in this world or any other that can keep us apart if you will be my wife."

Elizabeth sniffled and let out a deep, steadying breath. Her grip on his hand tightened and he could see her fight back her emotions. "Simon. When I was a little girl, I believed in fairy tales and magic. I believed in the impossible. Even when people said none of it was real, I still believed. And I searched. And from the fifth row, seat 26 in Hadley Hall, I found it. I found you. *You* are magic to me. What we have is magic. And you are all the proof I'll ever need to believe in the impossible. I loved you that first day. I love you now, here, today. And I will love you tomorrow and every tomorrow to come."

If Simon could have, he would have stopped the world then. It was a perfect moment in time. The Justice of the Peace cleared his throat and drew Simon and Elizabeth's attention back to him. The rest of the formalities were a blur. The only thing Simon would remember was the way she looked and the way she looked at him.

"You may now kiss the bride."

Simon didn't need to be reminded. He took Elizabeth into his arms and kissed his wife.

ELIZABETH CLOSED HER EYES and listened to Simon's heart beat out a steady, strong rhythm as the limousine drove them back home from the wedding. Their home. It felt a little odd to think of it that way. The house was so very Simon. But now, Simon was so very much hers too.

She opened her eyes just as the car pulled up front and stopped.

Simon kissed her temple. "Ready, Mrs. Cross?"

She heard the intensity of emotion behind the lighthearted question. "Very."

Simon stepped out of the car and held out his hand to help her. She took it and he gently pulled her up to his side. The sun had set over an hour ago and she felt the start of the night's chill in the air as they walked to the front door.

Simon unlocked the door and pushed it open. Before Elizabeth could wonder if he was going to carry her inside, he swept her off her feet and walked across the threshold. Once inside, he held her in his arms for a long moment. The depth of his love for her always took her breath away. His arms tightened around her urging her to lean up just enough for their lips to meet in a kiss.

He set her down gently and caressed her cheek. "I have something for you."

Elizabeth couldn't help herself and arched an eyebrow.

He chuckled and led her into the living room. "That too," he said, "but first just a small wedding gift."

"You didn't have to do that," Elizabeth protested as Simon opened a cabinet in a seldom-used credenza.

He pulled out a gift box and held it out to her. "I wanted to."

Elizabeth took the box, which was about the size of breadbox, and set it down on a small table. It was light and far too big for jewelry, which she seldom wore anyway. "What is it?"

He looked purposefully at the box as if it say, *open it and find out.*

She flipped back the lid and inside, nestled into white satin cushioning was a small stuffed tiger. It was old. Very old, from the Twenties. The stiches were loose and pulling apart. And it was the most beautiful thing she'd ever seen.

Tears filled her eyes as she remembered their first kiss. On Coney Island, when they'd traveled back to 1929, Simon had won her a small stuffed tiger, exactly like this one, and she'd left it behind in anger after their argument.

"He's not the same, I'm afraid," Simon said. "But I'm not the same man either."

He eased her around to look at him. "I pushed you away then and now I can't imagine letting go."

Exactly as she had that first time, Elizabeth steadied herself on Simon's shoulder and leaned up to kiss him. It was just the barest caress on the corner of his mouth at first before pulling away to look into his eyes. There was nothing tentative or unsure in the man who looked back at her this time. He was hers and she was his. And that was how it was meant to be.

Chapter Two

Simon collapsed onto the bed next to Elizabeth and pulled her into his arms. He felt the hot, quick brush of her breaths across his bare chest as she laid her head on his shoulder. They'd stayed in bed for a truly indecent amount of time over the last two days. He didn't remember ever having been so damn happy or, frankly, exhausted in all of his life.

Elizabeth sighed happily. "I think that was a record," she said still a little breathless.

Simon laughed and pushed his head back into the pillow. This was bliss. He'd never really understood the meaning until now. Lying in bed with his wife in his arms, breathless, that was truly bliss.

Elizabeth's arm rested on his chest and he knew she could feel the pounding of his heart. He covered her hand with his and wondered why they couldn't just stay like this forever.

He closed his eyes and was just giving himself over to the fantasy when the doorbell rang downstairs. "Damn it."

Elizabeth pushed herself up onto one elbow. "Expecting someone?"

"If that's Jack…" Simon said, his bliss long forgotten.

Elizabeth started to slip out from under the covers. "I'll go."

Simon caught her arm. "Not looking like that, you're not."

She laughed and turned back. "I was going to put on a robe."

"I should hope so," Simon said with a quirk of his lips, "but that's not what I meant." He gently urged her to lie back down. "I know I have to share you with the rest of the world, but this," he said as he caressed her face. "When your cheeks are flush with desire, your lips swollen from my kisses," he added as he gently traced the outline of her mouth, "I want this to be mine alone."

Elizabeth's slowing breath quickened. She nodded as she reached up to touch the back of his neck and pull him toward her. The doorbell rang again. This time, followed by a loud knocking.

Simon grunted and rolled out of bed. He put on his robe and strode downstairs.

He yanked open the door with such ferocity the deliveryman yelped in surprise. Simon's expression must have been as thunderous as he felt because the deliveryman actually took two steps back before muttering something about England.

Simon frowned and glared at the two workers on the path to his house, crates in mid-dolly. He'd nearly forgotten that he and Elizabeth had made arrangements for much of his grandfather's collection and books to be shipped from Hastings.

Simon tightened the sash on his robe and stepped aside. "All right. Put them over there."

The men wheeled in two large wooden crates and deposited them in the living room. Simon found some money in a drawer in the hall table, tipped them and sent them on their way as quickly as possible.

He looked at the crates as he made his way toward the stairs and hoped they might hold the answers to some of the questions that plagued him about his grandfather. Simon and Elizabeth barely had time enough to go through one tenth of his grandfather's things when they'd been in England. Now that they'd arrived, he felt the urge to explore again.

"Simon?" Elizabeth's voice filtered down from upstairs.

There were, however, other mysteries far more worthy of exploration at the moment, he thought with a smile. Crates temporarily forgotten, Simon started up the stairs again to return to his wife.

THE NEXT MORNING AFTER breakfast, Elizabeth's curiosity led her from the kitchen into the living room. She ran a hand over the rough wood of the crate and felt Simon come up behind her. "Should we?"

They were scheduled to leave on their honeymoon tour of Europe tomorrow. When they'd get back, the new semester would start and life would be normal again. She felt a strange pang at the idea. Normal was so…normal.

Simon came to her side. "Perhaps we should wait until we return."

Elizabeth fingered the edge of a crate. It was like putting out Christmas presents and saying you should wait until New Year's. "We could just go through this one. I'm practically packed."

Simon frowned; she knew he understood what practically packed really meant. But, she also knew he wanted to explore it as much as she did.

She looked up at him hopefully and he nodded. "I'll find something to open them with."

Simon found a hammer and used the claw to pry off the lid of one of the crates. He set it aside and Elizabeth reached into the shredded paper used for cushioning and pulled out one of Sebastian's treasures, a wooden carving of a tiny giraffe.

Simon came to her side and she handed him the small figure. "This all feels a little familiar, doesn't it?" he said, gesturing to the open crate.

"I'll say." It was more than familiar. One night more than a year ago now, Elizabeth had walked up to Simon's house to deliver a stack of graded papers. A set of Sebastian's things had arrived that day, too. In one of the boxes was the watch, the watch that sent them back in time, the watch that brought them together.

Simon's grandfather Sebastian, they'd discovered, was a time traveler who worked for something called the Council for Temporal Studies with a specialty in the Occult. It had been a lifelong secret until she and Simon had discovered his pocket watch, his time machine, and accidentally sent themselves to 1929 New York.

After surviving that trip, barely, they'd traveled twice more—once to 1906 San Francisco to save a man's life, and Simon's in the bargain, and then again to 1942 London to help a friend and fellow traveler, Evan Eldridge, lost in time. That's where they'd met Jack.

After completing their mission and dropping off Evan in 1906, Simon and Elizabeth returned to present day Hastings. Once there, arrangements were made for the contents of Sebastian's study to be sent to California. Getting themselves back to California wasn't so simple. Not being able to travel via conventional means due to Jack's complete lack of any modern-day ID, the three traveled directly to Santa Barbara, thanks to the watch and key Teddy Fiske had made for Elizabeth. And now, finally, the contents of Sebastian's study had caught up with them.

Inside the crate on the top level they found several books by Flemish alchemist John Fontaine, a stone bound with fine gold twine, and a Cleromancy kit. Elizabeth opened the small leather pouch and poured the contents into her hand. She set aside the dozen or so black and white beans and studied the two bone-carved dice with various runes on each side.

The divination by casting random lots was an ancient practice that transcended geography. From the Chinese I-Ching to ancient Rome, many cultures practiced some variation on the theme.

Elizabeth put the beans and dice back into the bag and dug into the crate. "Sebastian really got around, didn't he?"

Simon wrapped the small African fetish he'd been holding in a rough, colorful cloth and set it on the table. "Yes," Simon said. "So many different times and places."

Sebastian's adventures must have been incredible, Elizabeth thought, as they unwrapped one mysterious item after the next. She'd read some of Sebastian's papers on the occult, but they couldn't capture the feeling of holding an actual mystical artifact in your hand. She started to open a small ivory box, but stopped and looked to Simon when she heard him let out a short, quick breath.

He sat forward on the sofa, elbows coming to rest on his knees, a worn red leather book in his hands.

"Simon?"

He looked up and his eyes were bright with excitement and emotion. He held up the book. "His journal."

Elizabeth scooted down the sofa to sit at his side. "Have you seen that before?"

He shook his head and turned the book over in his hands. It was well-worn red leather with faded gold lettering that read: Chronicles. Simon picked up a dust jacket and handed it to Elizabeth. "It was hidden inside this."

"*Just So Stories*," Elizabeth read. "Kipling?"

Simon smiled at a fond memory. "He used to read them to me when I was very small, years before he started telling me his other stories."

Sebastian's "other stories" were wild accounts of things like his brunch with the Death Eaters of Peru and fighting zombies in eighteenth century Paris—fanciful tales that just happened to be true. Stories that had led to the amazing collection they had in front of them.

Sebastian's watch had let them travel through time, but the origin of the Council and its true purpose and even Sebastian's involvement remained a mystery. Elizabeth looked down at the book in Simon's hand. Until now. Maybe.

"He must have meant for you and no else to find it. Why else would he have put that dust jacket on it?"

Simon nodded, but kept his eyes on the book. Elizabeth knew memories of his grandfather were bittersweet. Sebastian died saving Simon's life and it was a guilt Simon carried with him to this day.

Elizabeth inched closer to him and rested a hand on his back. She could feel the tension in his muscles. "We don't have to do this now."

Simon huffed out a breath, turned to her and offered a reassuring smile. "It's all right. As you say, he meant for me to find this. Now, let's find out why."

Elizabeth tucked up her legs underneath her as she settled into the sofa and listened to Simon's deep, rich voice read Sebastian's journal. They spent the next few hours going through it. The book chronicled most of Sebastian's adventures in wonderful detail. He was a vivid storyteller and his passion for his work bled through every page.

"Despite all I have seen in my travels," Simon read, "I am still staggered to my very core at that moment when the impossible becomes real. The rabbi folded the piece of parchment upon which he had written the word '*shem*', a truncated version of one of the Kabbalistic names for the divine, and placed the paper into the Golem's mouth."

Despite the fact that this had happened years ago, hundreds of years ago according Sebastian's journal, Elizabeth still shivered at the image of the large, clay human figure of the Golem waiting to be brought to life.

"The rabbi spoke words so softly to the creature, I could not hear them, but the Golem did and he lurched forward, the inanimate animated."

Elizabeth felt herself leaning in, enraptured by the story.

"Under the rabbi's careful guidance, the Golem performed menial physical tasks, cleaning and carrying heavy objects and the like. The creature was well under his control, until that fateful night he forgot to remove the parchment from its mouth. It was a miracle the rabbi wasn't killed. He surely would have been had I not been there that night."

Simon peered over the top of the journal and caught Elizabeth's eyes. He arched both eyebrows in surprise and pleasure and then resumed reading. "To this very day, no man has dared set foot in the attic of that synagogue in Prague again."

After Simon read the last entry, a visit to ancient Mesopotamia, he closed the book and rested it on his knee. "He told me some of these stories when I was a boy," he said. "If only I'd known then that they were true."

"He certainly was far from the silent observer in some of those," Elizabeth said. There had been several adventures where Sebastian had consciously interfered. In fact, in some of them, the reason he'd gone there in the first place appeared to be to save someone's life.

"Yes, the non-interference edict he mentioned from the Council doesn't appear to always apply, does it?"

She reached for the book. "May I?"

Simon turned and the book slid off his knee and onto the floor.

"I'm sorry." Elizabeth moved forward to retrieve the book. "Is it okay?"

Simon picked up the book and surveyed it for damage. "No harm done."

Elizabeth let out a sigh of relief and as she moved back into the sofa, she noticed a piece of paper had fallen out from between the pages. She reached down and picked it up. "This fell out," she said as she held it out to Simon.

He took the paper and unfolded it. The air in the room went suddenly still.

Elizabeth leaned closer to see. It was a list with a dozen or so names with dates and locations. The first entry on the list made Elizabeth's blood run cold.

Manchester Arms, New York City, 4 PM August 20, 1929—Simon Cross.

CHAPTER THREE

"WHAT IS THIS?" ELIZABETH asked, a feeling of unease welling inside her. "Why on earth is your name on this list?"

Simon stared down at the piece of paper as shocked as she was. "This is just a few days before he saved my life."

"Saved both of our lives."

Simon pushed himself off the sofa. Pacing was a good idea. Elizabeth was tempted to join him, but seeing this list ripped open an old wound for Simon and now he would need his space. Simon strode back and forth, reading and rereading the list.

When she and Simon had gone back to 1929, the gangster King Kashian kidnapped her. Simon rushed after her and would have been killed if Sebastian hadn't come to his rescue at the very last second. Sebastian had died saving Simon, died in his arms, and the memory of that day still haunted him.

But Sebastian hadn't been there for Simon. At least that's what he'd told him. Elizabeth tried to reason it aloud. "When Sebastian found you, he told you he was there to study King."

"Yes, that's what he said."

The pain in his voice at the memories cut right to Elizabeth's heart. She stood and came to his side. He looked down at her and she could see he was trying hard to rein in his feelings. She put a supportive hand on his back and they both turned back to the paper in his hands.

At the top of the handwritten list in the left hand corner was the name "Cross" and to the right of that above the names, "*in absentia luci, tenebrae vincunt.*"

"What does that say?" she asked.

Simon furrowed his brow as he translated the Latin phrase. "In the absence of light, darkness prevails."

"That sounds like some sort of motto or creed," Elizabeth said. "I don't recognize it though."

Simon nodded, deep in thought.

"Maybe these were assignments from the Council," Elizabeth offered. "Like the rabbi and the Golem? Light and darkness."

"Possibly," Simon said.

"Look at the handwriting. All the other names and dates were written by the same hand, but your entry, it's slightly different. It's not quite the same."

Simon pulled himself out of the past with an effort and stared down at the list. "It's all his handwriting, but the spacing is odd, as though it was added to the top of the list after the others were written."

"Maybe Sebastian found out you were going to be in danger and put you to the top of the list?"

Simon ran a hand through his hair and massaged the back of his neck. "But how did he find out? And who are these others on the list? What's the connection between us?"

Elizabeth put a comforting hand on Simon's arm. "I don't know. Maybe the Council knows."

Simon's jaw clenched. Just the mention of the Council was enough to pique his anger. He'd always blamed them for his grandfather's death. Now, it seemed, there was more to it than just an assignment gone wrong.

"Sod the Council," Simon said under his breath. He glared down at the list, willing it to give him the answers he sought. "Grandfather meant for me to find this, not them. He wouldn't have hidden it in the Kipling dust jacket otherwise."

Simon stared at the yellowed piece of paper and then sat down heavily on the sofa. Elizabeth eased next to him and knew he was right. "This list meant something to him. It was important, important enough to hide from the Council. Important enough for him to risk his life."

Simon ran a hand through his hair and nodded his head. "Yes."

"These other names. Do any of them mean anything to you?" The names on the list felt random. The dates and locations spanned centuries and continents.

"No, I don't think so," Simon said.

"Maybe they're all like you were? In danger from the dark? King certainly qualifies."

"Yes," he said with a deep frown. Simon hardly needed to be reminded of what King was or what he'd done.

"Yes, but Council rules are strict on non-interference; he was firm about that."

"But then he did a fair amount of interfering, didn't he? With the Rabbi? With others? With you? And thank God he did." Elizabeth put her hand on his leg. "I get the feeling the

Council has two sets of rules and they break either when it suits them. I don't trust them, but I trust your grandfather. If he made this list, it meant something to him. You meant everything to him."

"I'm hardly important," Simon said and waved off Elizabeth's reply. "In the grand scheme of things."

"I don't know. How many people have a watch? How many people in all of history have traveled through time? Dozens out of hundreds of millions? I'd say that makes you kind of important in the grand scheme of things."

As unlikely and uncomfortable as he found the idea, she could tell he was considering the possibility.

"Maybe these people are at risk from the darkness? That absence of light thing," Elizabeth continued. "Maybe the darkness is another way of saying some sort of occult phenomena that changes things, like King, like the Golem. Unbalances something. And Sebastian's list is a way to put things right? To light the darkness."

Both she and Simon thought about it for a moment as they stared at the list. It was terrifying and exhilarating to contemplate the idea. If there was some dark force that was unsettling the balance of the world... Sebastian had specialized in the occult, which definitely qualified as darkness. She and Simon had battled something dark and unearthly in New York, and again with Madame Petrovka and even the Shard.

"It's possible," Simon said, looking at the list.

Elizabeth grabbed her laptop and started researching the names on the list. It was clear it would take a lot more than some good Google-Fu to find out anything about most of them. One of the names could have been a French bakery owner or politician. Or maybe even an artist. Another name showed up in the search results for those lost in a disaster on the Mississippi. But, most of the other names brought up nothing. Considering the dates went back over two hundred years, it wasn't all that surprising. Unless the people were famous, it was unlikely there would be much in the way of records on the Internet.

There was one name, however, that Elizabeth recognized.

"This one," Elizabeth said suddenly, running her finger along the name under Simon's. "Alan Grant, Hollywood, I know that name. It might be a different Alan Grant, but…"

She did a quick search and brought up a large image of a still from a movie—a handsome man, with sandy blond hair and pencil thin mustache, in his early forties. He was dressed as a buccaneer and using a dagger to rip through a giant sail as he sped down toward the deck of a large ship. He had a giant cutlass in his other hand and a broad, gleeful, wicked grin on his face.

Simon frowned. "Surely, it must be another Alan Grant."

"*The Sword of the Seven Seas!* I loved that movie."

Simon's expression was so flat it was almost concave.

"Alan Grant? *The Lost Musketeer? Midnight Masquerade?* He was a huge star."

"I didn't watch many movies growing up. Once I was at school, it was mostly Monty Python."

"And big points for that," Elizabeth said. "But you don't know what you're missing. Those old movies, they were so much fun."

"At some point it must have stopped being fun for Mr. Grant or he wouldn't be on the list, would he?"

"True." Elizabeth did a quick search and found Grant's bio, but it wasn't very helpful. "His credits just stop."

"In 1933?"

Elizabeth nodded.

Simon folded the piece of paper with the list and leaned back into the sofa cushion, letting his neck rest against the back of it, and looked to the ceiling. He looked tired. Heck, he was tired; she was tired. They'd been at this for hours and hours, and the emotional toll of discovering his grandfather's real reason for traveling to New York was starting to show.

"It's late," Elizabeth said. "Why don't we go to bed and we can talk about it tomorrow."

"We leave for Europe tomorrow."

In the excitement of it all, she'd nearly forgotten about their honeymoon. "Right."

She nestled closer to Simon. He reflexively put his arm around her and she put her head on his shoulder. They both stayed silent and still for a few minutes.

Finally, Elizabeth said, "We don't have to go."

Simon lifted his head and peered down at her. "Are we talking about Europe or…"

"Either, both. I don't know." She sat up and turned to face him. "I know I'm always the one pressuring you to go. And I don't want to do that. Not with this. As unlike me as it is," she said with a grin, "I will go wherever you want to go. This one has to be your choice."

Simon took her hand and caressed it. Finally, his fingers traced the edges of her wedding ring. "No, it's *our* choice. Together?"

"Agreed." Elizabeth covered his hand with hers and then added, "You go first."

Simon laughed and brought her hand to his lips. "I'm torn. I feel as though I owe it to my grandfather to finish what he started, but I owe you so much more. I owe you a life."

"Just for a moment. Forget me; forget Sebastian. What do *you* want?"

Simon thought sincerely about the question for a moment and then said so softly Elizabeth could barely hear him, "I want to go."

He looked at her and his expression and voice grew stronger. "A good man died to give me a second chance. I don't want to waste it being a tourist, when I can make a difference. If there is truly a darkness out there, and I believe there is, I can't walk away knowing I could do something about it. I don't know why he chose these people or made this list, but I want to follow it. And I want you with me wherever it leads."

Elizabeth sat up a little straighter and smiled. "I was hoping you'd say that."

Simon tugged on his ear in thought as he debated their choice. "We could, of course, go to Europe and deal with this when we return. 1933 isn't going anywhere."

Elizabeth had considered that. "It would be like an itch we couldn't scratch though. We have a chance to live history, to be the light. The rest just kind of pales in comparison, doesn't it?"

"It will probably be dangerous."

"No doubt."

Simon frowned.

"We still have Teddy's key," she said. Teddy Fiske's key allowed them to travel with the watch at will instead of waiting for an eclipse. It had saved their lives in London. "And it's not like there's a war going on or vampires lurking about."

"That we know of."

"Good point."

Simon shifted to face her. "Who knows what sort of dangers Alan Grant faces; what sort of darkness there is there?"

Elizabeth smiled. "It's a good thing you're an expert then, isn't it?"

Simon tried to frown, but couldn't quite manage it. "We don't know anything about that time."

"Ah," Elizabeth said with a widening grin. "But we know someone who does."

SIMON FOLDED HIS ARMS and leaned back against the kitchen

counter. "It's a terrible idea."

Jack expected that. Cross was full of don'ts and shouldn'ts and you'll put an eye outs. But, they needed him. He could sense it. And, if he were honest, he needed them.

Since they'd saved his life in 1942 and brought him back to the future with them, his life had been a series of amazements. The future was a lot to take in for a man from the forties.

They'd offered to return him to his own time. They could have safely deposited him away from the fire that nearly killed them all at Madame Tussauds and he could have resumed his life there. But, Jack was above all else, an adventurer and he couldn't pass up the opportunity to explore the future. And, if he were honest, three years of war had taken their toll. The Navy and then the OSS had been a great adventure, but war was, as they say, hell. And he didn't relish the idea of going back to it. After all, according to the history books, the good guys had won that one. They didn't need him. No one did really. It was an odd feeling for someone who was used to being indispensable.

The future had plenty going for it though. He might find a place here. Eventually. It was all he'd ever imagined and more. Buck Rogers had nothing on NASA. Man walked on the moon, talked to each other on phones without wires and waged war in ways he would have rather not known.

"I don't think it's wise," Simon said as he leaned back against his kitchen counter and crossed his arms over his chest.

"I can help," Jack said, hoping he could get through to him. "If this darkness or whatever you call it is real, don't you think having back up is a good idea?"

Simon frowned and spoke as though he were addressing a small, backwards child. "Need I remind you that there is already a *you* there?"

Jack frowned and chewed his lip. "Ah-ha!" he said, waving his finger in the air triumphantly. "You said April."

Simon's eyes narrowed. "I did."

Jack grinned. "I'm not there. I mean, I'm there, just not right there then, at that moment. In April 1933 I was getting the hell beat out of me in Arizona filming *The Dirtiest Trail* and *Si Si Senorita*." He opened his mouth as wide as it would go and pointed inside it. "I even lost a tooth."

"As compelling an argument as your missing tooth is," Simon said, "It's still too much of a risk. If you should alter the course of your own life…"

"What?" Jack said, worried for the first time.

"The repercussions could be disastrous. You could cease to be or worse."

"What's worse that?" Jack said.

Before Simon could give him a list of things that were more important than he was, Elizabeth stepped in. "If he's careful to avoid places he used to go and keeps a low profile, it could be pretty helpful to have someone there who knows what is what."

Jack gave Elizabeth a thankful smile. She was a good kid and, he knew, she understood him. She knew he needed more than being a sightseer in the future or a relic in the past. He needed to matter again.

"I could be helpful," Jack offered. "I *want* to be helpful. I'm not the kind of man who can sit still, you know, especially if there's something out there that needs doing. If there is a darkness like you said, I want to do something about it as much as you do."

Simon might be a pain in the posterior sometimes, but he was an honorable guy and he respected that in others. Jack could see from Simon's expression that he had a chance. "I don't know…"

35

"Simon, if Jack promised to avoid his usual haunts and women," she said with a pointed glare at Jack, "he could be a huge asset. He is a trained spy, after all. He knows the town; he knows the studio. We might need help just getting close to Alan Grant. Think of him like a time Sherpa."

"If things go sideways," Jack said, playing his trump card. "And let's face it, the odds are pretty good they will with her along."

"Hey!"

Simon nodded, conceding the point.

"She's got a gift for finding trouble."

"Yes, she does," Simon said.

Elizabeth waved her hand. "Standing *right* here."

Jack smiled apologetically. He loved her like a little sister and more than needing something to do, needing to feel useful again; he wanted to make sure she made it back in one piece. "Having a little backup might be—"

"Prudent." Simon agreed and pursed his lips in thought.

"Still here," Elizabeth muttered.

Simon frowned. "I'm sorry. I didn't mean any of that as a commentary on your abilities. It's just that we...worry."

Her indignation fizzled in the face of Simon's obvious and genuine concern. "Yeah, I know," she said.

"Good. And you understand about the timeline," Simon said to Jack.

"Not really," Jack said.

Simon sighed and Jack grinned.

"So," he said, feeling good to be back in the saddle. "When do we leave?"

Chapter Four

FOR THE NEXT WEEK they researched, planned and acquired. Thanks to their previous journeys, Simon had an extensive network of paper money collectors, and easily amassed more than enough money to last them for the duration, provided the duration wasn't more than a month. If it was longer, well, that meant they had bigger problems.

Elizabeth researched Alan Grant as best she could, but despite the Internet being the repository of human knowledge, there were significant gaps. Where Grant was concerned, it wasn't much help at all. She knew his favorite meal, which according to Photoplay was a dry martini, his favorite color, blue and his fascination with violin virtuoso, Niccolò Paganini. What neither the magazine, nor any other source, could tell her was what the heck happened to him.

Alan Grant was at the peak of a wildly successful film career with Mammoth Studios when he just disappeared. As far as she could tell, no official investigation or police report had been filed. Just a few mentions in the trades and then nothing; the world moved on to fixate on another star. Even what little she could learn about his personal life was hardly personal. But then, that wasn't all that surprising. During the heyday of the studio star system the lines between what was real and what the publicity department said was real were permanently blurred.

Other than that, they only had the date and location from Sebastian's list: 6 PM, April 6, 1933—Musso & Frank, Hollywood. Luckily, no earthquakes were scheduled; once was enough on that front, and no other major disasters loomed. The only significant event that week in Los Angeles was the repeal of the prohibition on beer.

Musso & Frank, a famous Hollywood restaurant, would be easy to find. It had been in the same spot for nearly 100 years. But what threatened Alan Grant was still a mystery. All they could do now was go back and find out.

Elizabeth felt excited at the idea. She'd been excited when they'd traveled to 1906 San Francisco and even when they'd headed into war-torn 1942 London on their last trip. But the idea of going back to Hollywood during the Golden Age was an honest to goodness thrill. She'd spent hours watching old movies in dingy hotel rooms all across Texas as a little girl. Everything always seemed so magical, so possible in the movies. And, of course, she was a sucker for a happy ending. Those late nights she'd spent waiting for her father to come home from a night of gambling were lonely and the movies had kept her company. The films and their stars, especially the swashbuckling adventurers like Douglas Fairbanks, Errol Flynn, and Alan Grant, always had a special place in her heart. Having the chance to pay him back somehow made this trip all the more important to her.

Satisfied they couldn't learn any more without actually being there, they decided to leave Saturday morning. Clothes bought and packed, Simon's tea tucked into one of the side pockets of their suitcase, the three got dressed for their parts. Luckily, April in Los Angeles meant balmy weather, but then so did October and December. Elizabeth wore a light floral dress with comfortable, genuinely comfortable, shoes this time. Jack looked like an ad for the Great Gatsby in his baggy, cream-colored linen pants and snug baby blue polo sweater. Simon looked extra sexy in his grey double-breasted suit, the sleeves of his white oxford shirt rolled up to mid-forearm and his jacket casually slung over one arm.

"Why do men always look so good in period clothes?" Elizabeth asked as Simon pulled down the brim of his fedora.

"Have you looked in the mirror?" Simon said with an appreciative glance at her figure.

"He's right," Jack said. "You look…" His voice trailed off as Simon patiently and curiously waited for him to finish. "Um… like a beautiful, but very married woman." Jack picked up their suitcases as the corner of his mouth quirked into a smile.

Simon chuckled and made sure the watch settings were correct. He went over the date and location again to make sure they were accurate and then asked, "Everyone ready?"

Elizabeth took the key from around her neck and handed it to Simon. She took hold of Jack's hand and gripped Simon's arm with the other.

Simon gave them all one last look to make sure all was well before putting the key into the hole in the watch and turning it. Seconds later, the electric blue light snaked out of the watch and up his arm. Almost instantly, all three of them were caught in its web and the world shook itself apart.

IT WAS JUST AFTER three o'clock on April 5, 1933, when they arrived in Jack's small apartment on Franklin Avenue near the base of the Hollywood Hills. After a lengthy discussion on the safest place to arrive unseen, they'd all settled on Jack's apartment. Once the coast was clear, they'd leave and head for hotels away from his usual stomping ground.

Jack's place was a charming one bedroom upstairs in the Spanish Revival-style complex that was so popular in Los Angeles in the late 20's and early 30's. As soon as the world righted itself, Elizabeth heard the sound of a piano through the thick adobe-like walls. Whoever was playing hit a sour note.

"That's Billy, he's actually getting better," Jack said, rubbing his temple. "Like you said; not as bad this time."

Elizabeth remembered the first time she'd time traveled. She thought her head was going to fall off her shoulders. "It gets easier each time."

Jack's apartment was small, but surprisingly clean for a bachelor's. The floor was a beautiful light-colored wood with a darker inlay around the edges. All of the doorways were arched and open. And the mid-day sun streamed through the windows in the kitchen and front room. Every inch of it had personality. Elizabeth wondered when apartments became like her old place, just a series of dull little boxes. "Jack, your apartment is adorable."

"Exactly what I was going for," he said looking around skeptically.

"Lookin' good, Junie!" a shrill woman's voice called from outside.

Simon discreetly peered through the curtain sheers of the front window.

"Don't worry, that's just Hilde," Jack said.

In the courtyard below, a woman with short shorts and a bikini top waved to a little girl who practiced her buck and wing under the eagle eye of her plump, hovering mother. Two middle-aged men wearing matching shirts and matching faces played what looked like a very serious game of checkers, while a third man lay on his back on the edge of the courtyard fountain with sketchpad in hand.

"Is it always so busy?" Simon asked.

Jack peered through the curtains briefly. "Yeah, that's pretty much the usual gang for a weekday. People without jobs have a lot of free time."

To Elizabeth, the Great Depression always conjured images of people in soup lines in New York or hardscrabble farmers in the Dust Bowl. It was easy to forget that every part of the country was affected.

Jack walked across the small living room and into the open kitchen. He opened the door to the squat refrigerator that had a big cylindrical compressor on top making the whole thing look like a retro robot. He bent down and pulled out a bowl of something, smelled it, made a face and quickly put it back in and closed the door.

"We should go as soon as we're able," Simon said. "We need to get settled at the hotel. Pardon me, hotels," Simon added with a frown as he lingered over the s in hotels.

Jack rubbed his face. "Yeah, sorry about that, but it's better if I don't run into Ruth."

Jack had had an affair with a woman at the Ambassador Hotel and, Elizabeth had the feeling, timeline aside, Jack wanted to avoid seeing Ruth again.

"Besides," Jack said. "I don't need anything fancy like the Ambassador. The El Rey'll do me just fine."

Simon was about to argue the point, again, when Elizabeth shook her head at him, asking him silently to let it be. Elizabeth had a feeling it wasn't just Ruth that made Jack uncomfortable. With no money to his name, Jack had been beholden to Simon for everything. It was hard enough for him to accept the money he needed to live, without adding a luxury hotel into the mix.

"Alley's clear," Jack said. "I'll call a cab and we can sneak out the back."

While Jack made the call, Simon reviewed their plan. They would check into the hotels and get settled. After dinner, they'd start seeing what they could learn about Alan Grant.

According to a *Modern Screen* "Behind the Scenes with Alan Grant" article Elizabeth had found online, Grant was a frequent visitor to many of Los Angeles' best nightclubs. Lucky for them, one of the most popular clubs, the Cocoanut Grove, was right in their hotel. It was as good a place as any to start.

"Okay," Jack said. "Cab'll come by Franklin and La Brea in a few minutes."

"Good," Simon said, as he picked up their suitcase. "Can we go out the back door?" He nodded toward the door in the kitchen.

"Yeah, just one thing," Jack said holding up a finger. He disappeared into what Elizabeth assumed was the bedroom and came back out carrying a metal box. He set it down on the kitchen counter and pulled out something wrapped in a cloth.

A gun. He flicked open the cylinder to make sure it was empty and snapped it closed.

"Just in case," he said as he tucked the gun into his jacket pocket and poured a handful of bullets into the other.

It was a sharp reminder of what they might face. As excited as Elizabeth was to be here, the danger they faced was real. Judging from Simon's grim expression, he was thinking the same thing.

Jack checked to make sure the alley was clear once again and the trio made their way down the back stairs and out into 1933.

LOS ANGELES WAS UNLIKE most other major cities; it didn't grow vertically like New York, it grew horizontally, spreading out over hundreds of square miles. In 1930 it was half orange groves and half upstart metropolis. Despite the Depression, Elizabeth saw signs of new construction everywhere. Los Angeles wasn't just about a place to live; it was about transformation. Nothing, including most of the people, was native. Even most of the ubiquitous palm trees had come from somewhere else to help transform the desert into a dream.

Driving through Los Angeles in 1930 was like peeking into the dressing room of a star with only half her make-up on—blotchy and uneven, but a promise of seductive beauty just around the corner.

Elizabeth rolled down the window in the enormous back seat of the cab and tried to get a better look. Even though it was still fairly early days for the automobile, they were everywhere in Los Angeles. And nearly every car in the thirties seemed big enough to house a small family.

Their behemoth taxi drove down Western Avenue from the hilly residential section of the Hollywood foothills into the heart of Los Angeles. They came to a stop at Hollywood Boulevard and one of the Pacific Electric Red Cars, a large sprawling network of trollies and light rail, rumbled past. Sadly, the Red Cars' days were numbered and the automobile would soon supplant just about every form of public transportation in Los Angeles.

Their cab crossed Sunset Boulevard and passed Paramount-Famous Lasky Studios and down to Wilshire Boulevard where Hollywood came to eat and play.

"Look," Elizabeth said. "The Brown Derby." Although the Brown Derby had several locations, this was the most famous. The restaurant was shaped like its namesake, a huge brown derby, brim and all. "We have got to go there."

Simon smiled. "If we have time."

The cab turned away from the Derby and that's when Elizabeth saw the Ambassador Hotel. Before it became infamous for being the site of Robert F. Kennedy's assassination, it was one of the premiere hotels in Los Angeles. No wonder. It was enormous and gorgeous. A huge perfectly manicured lawn stretched out for hundreds of feet in front of the over 500-room hotel. The cab entered along the side entrance and under an overhang that protected people from imaginary Los Angeles rain.

As Simon paid the driver, giving him enough to take Jack to his hotel downtown, Elizabeth made arrangements with Jack to check in with each other in the morning. She slipped him a handful of money, knowing he'd be reluctant to take anything else from Simon.

"Take it. You never know," Elizabeth said.

Jack frowned. "I hate this."

"I know," she said and kissed his cheek. "Stay out of trouble."

"That's my line," he said. Elizabeth smiled and he grew serious for a moment. "I've kinda grown attached to you. Even him."

"Even me?" Simon said from behind them.

Jack smirked. "I'll see ya tomorrow."

He climbed back into the cab and Simon and Elizabeth walked into the hotel. After Simon arranged for a room, a bellhop, in full organ grinder monkey regalia, ran up to them, smiled and took their bag. "This way, please."

Instead of leading them to the large bank of elevators, he led them through the lobby, past shops and a large restaurant, past the signs that announced Bing Crosby was appearing at the Cocoanut Grove that week and out of the back of the hotel. For his part, Simon didn't look surprised and was maybe even a little pleased with himself.

They walked out into the bright California sunshine and around a large swimming pool complete with a sandy beach and large clubhouse. The scent of lemon and orange blossoms hung in the warm air. In the distance, Elizabeth could see what looked like a miniature golf course. They walked down a set of stairs and into a lush garden. Elizabeth was just beginning to wonder where the heck he was leading them when she saw pergolas covered with bougainvillea along the paths between what looked like private houses.

Finally, the bellboy stopped in front of number seven and opened the door for them. "Mr. & Mrs. Cross," he said, gesturing for them to go first, "your bungalow."

Bungalow sounded like it was a cute little one-room job or a thatched hut for Moon Doggie and Gidget. This was more like something for Elizabeth Taylor and Richard Burton. The bungalow was really just a luxurious house for rent on the hotel property. It had a beautifully decorated living room, kitchen, dining room and even an upstairs. As Simon tipped the boy and made arrangements to have their clothes pressed for tonight, Elizabeth explored the second floor. The upper floor held the spacious master bedroom suite and a balcony that overlooked the grounds. She pulled open the large French doors and stepped out to breathe in the warm spring air with just a hint of jasmine in it.

After a few minutes, she heard Simon come upstairs and felt him standing behind her. She turned and leaned back against the railing with both elbows. "This is amazing."

Simon hmm'd in agreement, but from the look in his eye he wasn't thinking about the bungalow. Slowly, he walked over to her, stopping just inches away from her. He put a hand on either side of her on the railing, trapping her between his arms.

"We have a few hours before dinner," Simon whispered in her ear. "I have ideas for one of them. Perhaps you can think of something for the others, Mrs. Cross?"

Oh, she had ideas. Plenty of ideas.

ELIZABETH STARED UP AT the ceiling of the Cocoanut Grove in wonder. A detailed firmament of stars sparkled against the midnight blue paint. Small spotlights were mixed amongst the stars and lit the enormous floor of the supper club. She and Simon stood near one of the many life-sized palm trees that ringed the perimeter of the main floor. Nestled at the base of the large fronds a small stuffed monkey dangled down next to a bunch of fake cocoanuts. Why weren't there places like this anymore?

Simon caught the attention of one of the maître 'ds and asked for a table on the upper level that ringed the main floor. The man bowed and led them through the club. It was bright and bilious—Hollywood's version of Morocco. Everything was deep, rich reds and golds. The walls were accented with sharp Moorish arches with detailed geometric designs and floral arabesques.

The man stopped at a small table near the steps down to the dance floor. He held out Elizabeth's chair and she took her seat.

"Who's here tonight?" Simon said casually, as though he asked the question regularly and expected a response.

The man hemmed a little until Simon pulled out his billfold. "Oh, yeah, there's uhm, Carole Lombard over there," he said nodding his head toward each star as he ticked off the night's visitors. Elizabeth strained to see them in the distance. It was clear the man was used to the question and used to getting a nice bit of change for the answer. "And, Gable and Shearer and Thalberg."

Simon handed him several bills. "And Grant? Alan Grant?"

The man shook his head. "Not yet. But it's kind of early for him."

"Thank you," Simon said, and held out one more bill. "You'll be sure to let us know if he should arrive."

"Very good, sir," he said as he took the last bit of compensation.

Simon took his seat just as the orchestra started to play and Bing Crosby took the stage. He opened with "Waltzing in a Dream." It was appropriate. The entire day had felt like a dream. She and Simon and Jack had arrived safely and without incident, which was a first for them. The hotel was beautiful and now she was sitting there listening to young Bing Crosby serenade her, live. The only thing missing was the only the reason they were there. Alan Grant.

They had dinner and waited. They had drinks and waited. They danced and waited. The evening came and went, but Grant did not. Eventually, they decided to give it up for the night and start fresh in the morning, hoping Jack might have had better luck.

As it turned out, he didn't. As promised, Jack called them in the morning, but he didn't have much to report. From what he'd learned from poking around, Grant spent his days at the studio or his home, neither of which they could get near, and his nights at any one of a few dozen nightclubs. That left Musso & Frank. At least they knew he'd be there and when. All they could hope for now was that whatever was threatening Grant, they'd be ready for it.

CHAPTER FIVE

MUSSO & FRANK WAS exactly as Elizabeth had imagined it. It was a dark, wood-paneled room with red leather booths and wall sconces that gave off a warm, reddish-orange glow. A long mahogany bar ran the length of one side of the deep and narrow restaurant. Jack sat on the last barstool, near the kitchen door, just as they'd planned. Jack had pointed out that it was better strategically if they weren't sitting together and didn't acknowledge each other. If trouble broke out, it would be better to have two angles on it.

Elizabeth saw Jack notice them at the front of the restaurant and nodded his head toward the back corner booth. That must be where Alan Grant was sitting. She nodded once, feeling like she was in *The Sting* and turned her attention away from Jack.

The restaurant was fairly large. In addition to the bar, various booths and tables filled the rest of the floor. It was steeped in movie history. Musso & Frank was a haven for Hollywood's elite and not just the stars, but writers, directors, producers and artists of all kinds. She could practically feel the buzz of deals being brokered and the electricity of ideas being born.

While she and Simon stood at the entrance, waiting for the maître d' to seat them, two men slid out of a nearby booth. The short one had stacks of papers clutched under his arms. His tweed jacket was rumpled and the rest of his clothes weren't in much better shape. He looked familiar. It was his short grey hair and near black mustache.

"Don't worry, Bill, it'll be all right," the other man assured him as they walked toward a back room.

Bill nodded, but he didn't seem convinced. "I hope so, Leland," he said with a deep, slow Southern drawl. "I surely hope so."

The two men disappeared up the back stairs and Elizabeth grabbed Simon's arm. "Holy crap. That was William Faulkner."

She'd read that he and F. Scott Fitzgerald and others sometimes wrote at Musso & Frank, but to actually see him! She barely managed to refrain from shouting after him, "*As I Lay Dying* was completely awesome!"

She turned around eagerly looking for the next literary icon.

"Hmm?" Simon said, staying on point and craning his neck to try to spot Alan Grant.

Elizabeth pulled her attention back to the task at hand. She wasn't here to sightsee or star gaze, she reminded herself. She was here for Alan Grant, and if their theories were right, he was about to be in big trouble. "Back corner booth. Down there," she whispered to Simon.

The maître d' approached and led them to a table, but it was too far away. Elizabeth touched Simon's arm and nodded toward a group of empty tables closer to the back corner.

"I'd prefer somewhere with a bit more privacy," Simon said. "Perhaps, that one?"

The maître 'd shook his head apologetically. "I'm sorry, sir, those tables are reserved."

"It's our honeymoon," Simon said as he deftly palmed a five-dollar bribe and discreetly flashed it for the man to see.

"Congratulations," he said, shaking Simon's hand and taking the money in one fluid motion. "In that case, we would be happy to make an exception."

He led them to the back part of the restaurant.

"That's him," Elizabeth said under her breath as they neared a large booth with four men and a woman.

"This one will do nicely," Simon said choosing a table close to Grant's.

Elizabeth slid into the booth, making sure she had a good view of Grant's table. The large partition at the back of her booth blocked any chance of seeing Jack again. She just had to hope he could see Grant well enough to intervene if it came to that.

Alan Grant looked exactly like he did in the movies, except now; in place of his roguish smile there was a serious, even worried expression. And he wasn't alone.

In addition to Grant, there were four others in the large crescent-shaped booth, three men and a young woman. Grant sat next to a lanky, but attractive man in his mid-fifties. His brown hair was smoothed back accentuating his already sharp features. He sat back casually in his seat, but Elizabeth could see the intensity in his eyes as he watched the others. It made him seem vaguely hawk-like and predatory.

On Grant's other side sat a young woman. She couldn't have been much older than Elizabeth, mid-twenties at most.

She was the epitome of the young, platinum blonde starlet who should have had the world at her feet. And maybe she did, but not today. Her mascara ran down her cheeks and her eyes darted anxiously between the men in the booth. She looked pleadingly at the man to her right.

"Benny," she said to him, "what about me?"

Elizabeth could hear the desperation in her voice and cast a nervous glance at Simon. They'd obviously arrived in the middle of a tense discussion. So tense that the woman seemed to be near panic.

Benny frowned down at her with impatience and a little disgust before ignoring her completely. He needlessly ran a few fingers through the side of his perfectly arranged, slicked-back hair. From the slight, but permanent smirk on his lips to the broad pinstripes of his suit, it was clear Benny thought an awful lot of himself. He wasn't bad looking, if a little bit on the Cro-Magnon side of things. His brow was heavy set, almost thuggish and there was an air to his mannerism that Elizabeth recognized as coming from a man who usually got his way. Elizabeth knew she shouldn't make snap judgments and there were oodles of things she didn't know about these people, but she knew one thing: Benny was an ass.

The last man in the booth was an older one and pudgier than Benny, but the family resemblance was uncanny. Where Benny was probably in his mid-thirties, the man to his right had to be closer to sixty. Maybe he was his older brother or even his father? The older man worried the end of an unlit cigar as he glared through his round wire-rimmed glasses at the hawkish man next to Grant.

"You're sure these contracts are iron-clad?" he asked.

The hawkish man nodded his head and an odd smile quirked the corners of his mouth. While the others seemed to be in various states of panic, anger or despair, he was icily calm and even almost pleased.

As if he'd heard Elizabeth's thoughts, the hawkish man looked toward her and she dipped her head and pretended to be fascinated by her water glass. She could feel him looking at her and even felt the moment he looked away. Elizabeth shook off the spider-crawls inching up her spine and forced herself to look back to the table.

The young woman who had clearly been crying sniffled into her handkerchief loudly. "Ain't there nothin' we can do?" she pleaded to each of the men at the table, finally turning to the man with the thick brow, "Benny?"

She nuzzled closer to him, but he shrugged her off. Alan Grant laid a comforting hand over hers and smiled kindly. But Elizabeth could see that he was worried too. Were all of the people at the table in the same danger he was?

A black waistcoat and the waiter inside it suddenly obscured Elizabeth's view of the table. "Would you like to order something to drink?" he asked as he handed them their menus.

"Tea," Simon said reflexively.

"Hot tea," Elizabeth clarified. Prohibition meant restaurants had to disguise their drinks in teacups in case the police decided to snoop around. Musso & Frank's clientele was hardly the sort to go dry. After working at Charlie Blue's nightclub, she knew that ordering tea could get you a variety of bathtub liquors strong enough to strip paint off a wall. "I'll just have a water," she added.

The waiter didn't hide his disappointment and started to leave, but Alan Grant held up his empty teacup and the waiter nodded in understanding.

Simon dipped his head close to Elizabeth's. "Do you recognize any of the others?"

The older man with the glasses did look vaguely familiar, but she couldn't place him. "No, not really."

Simon nodded and sat up straight again. He kept a sharp watch around the rest of the restaurant. There was no telling what sort of danger Grant was in. It was best to stay alert and ready.

"Look," Benny said. "I got places to be." He looked at the older man to his right and then at the hawkish one. "This ain't over."

The hawkish man inclined his head and smiled with mild amusement.

Benny jerked his thumb toward the door. "Let's get outta here."

The older man shook his head and sighed, but slid out of the booth. The young woman watched them with fresh tears in her eyes. Benny gestured irritably for her to follow. "Come on."

She started to protest, but any backbone she might have had wilted under his impatient glare.

"It will be all right, Ruby," Alan said to her as she joined the others.

Ruby gave Alan a grateful, weepy smile and then hurried to keep up with the others as they left.

The hawkish man put his hands on the edge of the table and leaned back. He seemed very pleased with himself. "If there's nothing else?"

Grant laughed, but there was no joy in it. He shook his head. "No, I think…there is nothing else."

The other man nodded, slid out of the booth and tossed some bills on the table. Grant raised his cup in mock thanks as the man walked away leaving him alone.

As planned, Jack appeared near their booth then and dropped something on the floor. "Well?" he said under his breath as he knelt down to retrieve it.

"We'll stay," Elizabeth whispered. "See what you can learn about the others."

Jack nodded, picked up his keys and followed the hawkish man out of the restaurant.

The waiter came back and placed a fresh teacup and saucer in front of Grant.

"Bless you," Grant said as he took a deep drink from it.

His hand trembled as he put the teacup back onto the saucer. His soulful blue eyes squeezed shut and opened again after he let out a deep, shaky breath. He looked so tired and beaten. It was a look she never expected to see on him. It was silly. Of course, she knew he was flesh and blood, and not the larger than life hero she'd seen in so many movies. But seeing him up close like this, so wounded, was unnerving.

Grant looked up just in time to catch Elizabeth staring at him. She smiled back shyly, suddenly feeling like an awful intruder. A small smile curved Grant's mouth. He looked down into his cup and then back up again. The man was gone and the movie star was back in a flash of his broad smile. "Girl!"

Elizabeth felt her cheeks go hot and was sure they were as deep a red as the leather in the restaurant's booths. *Me?* she pantomimed, feeling every inch the fangirl she was.

"Yes, you!" Grant said loudly, his subtle, upper-class Transatlantic accent slightly dulled by drink. "Come here!" He waved her over to his booth.

Despite the fact that she was there on what could be a dangerous mission, Elizabeth suddenly felt giddy. She felt a huge smile wash over her face. She was being beckoned by Alan Grant. *The* Alan Grant. There was beckoning. She turned to Simon to share her excitement only to find him watching her with a bemused smile. Maybe she was making a fool of herself, but she didn't care.

"You can bring your…" Grant said with an indifferent wave in Simon's direction. "Come, come, come."

They did as he requested and she stood awkwardly at the edge of his table. He looked up at Elizabeth through red-rimmed eyes. "What is your name?"

"Elizabeth," she said, feeling like she'd stepped into a movie.

"Ah, Elizabeth!" he said, waving his hand expansively. "Fit for a queen and a chorus girl I knew once in Dubuque. Please join me?" he said and then added almost to himself. "I don't do well alone."

Elizabeth and Simon sat down. Alan rose slightly in a courtly bow, and extended a hand toward Simon. "And you are, sir?"

Simon shook his hand. "Simon Cross. My wife is a quite a fan of yours."

Grant perked up at that. "Is she? How wonderful!" He tried to rest his elbow on the edge of the table, but missed on the first try. Got it on the second. "Have you seen many of my pictures? They aren't all worth it, mind you, but some of them aren't bad."

Elizabeth could hardly believe she was sitting having drinks with Alan Grant. "I've seen them all."

Alan rested his chin on the palm of his hand and gazed at her. "Aren't you a dear?"

"I think I loved *The Sword of the Seven Seas* the most. When you asked Myrna Loy to leave Basil Rathbone and go with you…"

Alan grabbed Elizabeth's hand and pressed it to his chest. "Come with me, Lucia, across the seven seas and I will lay kingdom after kingdom, the riches of all the world, at your bejeweled feet." He finished with a flourish that nearly knocked over a water glass and kissed Elizabeth's hand.

All she could do was sigh. It was cheesy and ridiculous and absolutely wonderful. For his part, Simon looked slightly nauseated. Alan basked in the glow of the memory and Elizabeth's adoration for a moment before sighing dramatically. "That was a wonderful picture. They don't make movies like that anymore."

Elizabeth did some quick math. "It's only been two years."

"My darling, in the picture business that's a lifetime." His smile faded. "My lifetime."

Elizabeth knew it was awkward to ask, but she had to try. "If you don't mind my asking, who were those people you were with before? Some of them seemed upset."

Alan let himself wallow for a moment longer before answering her, his melancholy replaced with a new tension. "Nothing for you to worry about. Business associates. Roth and his brother are always stirring up some sort of trouble. But that's not for a beautiful woman like you to worry about," he said and then touched the tip of her nose. "The night is young and so are you!"

He raised his cup in a toast and drank the rest of the contents, at least two shots of liquor. Simon and Elizabeth exchanged amazed and slightly worried glances. After he drank, he slapped the table and his mood shifted yet again. He shed the cloud that hung over him and that mischievous spark lit his blue eyes again. "How would you like to have a little fun?"

ALAN'S CAR WAS WAITING out front and his chauffeur, a large, heavy-set black man, got out from behind the wheel and met them at the curb.

"Peter," Alan said, although it came out sounding like "pita", "I'd like you to meet Simon and Elizabeth Cross. They're going to join us for the evening."

Elizabeth reflexively stuck out her hand toward Peter. He looked at it, unsure for a moment. It was only then Elizabeth realized in this era, it was probably odd for a woman to shake hands, and even stranger to offer hers to a black man. Without meaning to, she'd forced Peter into a very uncomfortable position. But she couldn't take it back now and, frankly, didn't want to.

Peter looked briefly to Alan, who seemed more amused than anything else. Peter took off his cap, tucked it under one arm and shook her hand. "Ma'am."

Peter quickly let go of her hand, put his cap back on and opened the back door to Alan's forest green Bentley limousine. Elizabeth went in first and slid across the plush leather seat. Simon sat next to her and then Alan flopped into the seat opposite them. He lifted the top of a domed, silver cigarette holder bolted into the middle of the back seat floor and offered one to Elizabeth and then Simon before lighting one for himself. He rapped on the glass partition behind him. A moment later, Peter slid it open.

"Egyptian," Alan said and then checked his watch. "If we hurry, we can make the early show."

Peter slid the partition closed and Elizabeth felt the car rumble to a start.

Alan leaned back into his seat and blew smoke up to the high ceiling of the car.

"We're going to the movies?" Elizabeth asked.

Alan grinned. "Something like that."

A few minutes later they pulled up in front of the Egyptian Theatre on Hollywood Boulevard. Alan cleared his throat, smoothed down his hair and said, "It'll be more fun if you play along."

Just as Elizabeth was about to ask what that meant, Alan popped open the back door and jumped out of the car. He offered Elizabeth his hand in a silent request to join him.

"Be careful and stay alert," Simon said.

She nodded. They still had no idea what threat there was against Alan's life. Elizabeth took Alan's hand. He wrapped her arm in his and strode toward the box office like Caesar with Cleopatra at his side. She had to nearly run to keep up with him as he led her through the long Egyptian forecourt. Large potted palms and brightly painted Egyptian art lined the sandstone-like walls on either side of them as they neared the inset entrance to the theater.

Elizabeth could hear Simon behind them grumbling something about the hieroglyphics being utter nonsense. A couple lingering by one of the ornate fountains did a double-take as Alan strode past.

As they approached the front of the theater, a broad colonnade with four enormous columns, Elizabeth noticed a man pacing back and forth across the roof above the marquee. He was dressed as some sort of Egyptian guard. He stopped as he saw them and waved his ceremonial staff in greeting. "Mr. Grant!"

The young man in the ticket booth gasped as Alan walked past. He strained to see if his eyes were deceiving him and pressed his face up against the glass as Elizabeth and Alan walked under the marquee and toward the large double doors.

"M-Mr. Grant," stuttered the red uniformed man at the door.

"You don't mind if we slip inside, do you?" Alan asked. "Just to say hello."

"N-no!" the man said and stood aside.

"Good lad." Alan clapped him on the back and gestured for Elizabeth and Simon to go first.

Elizabeth had only read about theaters like this. The Egyptian theater was the very definition of a movie palace. Everything about it was elegant and opulent. From the plush carpet to the dazzling chandeliers, magnificent grand staircases to smartly-uniformed and attentive staff, every nuance was designed to make every patron feel like they were someone special, as if they were experiencing something magical. Egyptian motifs were everywhere. More hieroglyphics, these outlined in gold, ringed the high ceiling. Elizabeth tried not to giggle when she saw huge statues of the god of the underworld, Osiris, guarding the entrance to the ladies' bathroom.

Next to her, Simon snorted. "Ridiculous."

The three of them had barely taken more than two or three steps inside when a portly man in a broad-shouldered suit hurried over to them. He mopped his brow and stuffed his handkerchief in his pocket. He stuck out a meaty paw and Alan politely shook it.

"Mr. Grant," he said, almost panting for breath. "It's an honor to have you here."

"Thank you."

"Your picture's showin'. Right in there! Right now!"

Alan's mock surprise was priceless. "Is it really?" he turned and winked at Elizabeth.

"It is," the man said, his head bobbing in excitement. He glanced at his watch. "It should be letting out—"

The rest of his sentence wasn't necessary as four sets of double doors to the theater opened at once and a trickle of moviegoers soon became a mass. It only took a few seconds for one of them to recognize Alan Grant.

Two women called out Alan's name in unison, soon a few more followed and the rush was on.

"Stay close," Alan said in a hushed voice. "Sometimes I think they'd love me to death if they could."

Simon gripped Elizabeth's arm and leaned toward her. "We should get him out of here."

"I don't think we can."

In less than a minute, they were surrounded by Alan's adoring fans. He was gracious to each, signing autographs, shaking hands and being utterly surprised and delighted that they enjoyed his pictures.

Someone tapped Elizabeth on the shoulder and she turned to find a rosy-cheeked teenage girl, autograph book in hand. "Are you somebody?"

"Well, I—"

"Somebody?" Alan said with a booming laugh as he edged over to them. "My dear child, this…" he said loudly, sure to get everyone else's attention, and with a dramatic pause for effect, "…is Elizabeth Cross!"

The crowd ooh'd and aww'd as though they recognized the name. Before she could protest, programs and autograph books were being shoved toward her. She started to glare at Alan, but remembered his advice. It was definitely more fun if she played along. Alan took a moment and gave her a wicked and pleased grin before going back to signing autographs. Elizabeth shook her head. He was going to be trouble.

A young man asked Simon who he was, and Elizabeth prepared for a storm of poison arrows, but Simon just sighed, crossed his arms and said. "Her husband."

"Oh, he's nobody," the young man announced to the crowd. "Just her husband."

Elizabeth laughed at Simon's offended expression. "You're a somebody to me," she assured him.

Whatever tart reply he offered was lost as she was pulled around by yet another adoring, and instant fan.

After a few more whirlwind minutes, Alan made an abrupt, grand exit and they were safely back in the car. Elizabeth tried to catch her breath. The experience had been bizarre and exhilarating. Alan lounged in his seat and reached for an already prepared glass of whisky. Fans followed them out and rapped on the windows. Elizabeth looked over at Simon who plucked a slip of paper from the shoulder strap of her dress and arched an eyebrow. A phone number. When had someone done that? She smiled and shrugged. Simon merely shook his head and sighed.

Alan rapped on the partition and the car eased away from the crowd. He took a sip of his drink and grinned. "Now, *that* was fun!"

CHAPTER SIX

"A RE THOSE OIL DERRICKS?" Elizabeth peered out of the limousine window. The silhouettes of palm trees had given way to the unmistakable silhouettes of oil wells. And, not just one or two, but an entire forest of them.

"The only thing the city has more of than actors," Alan said, "is oil."

A few minutes later they rounded a corner and arrived at their next destination.

"Just saying hello to a few friends," Alan said casually as their car pulled up to the Biltmore Hotel.

As they got out of the car, Elizabeth noticed again how incredibly handsome Simon looked tonight and took hold of his hand. She knew this was hardly a vacation, but that didn't mean she couldn't enjoy being with her husband. Simon squeezed her hand and then wrapped it through his arm as they walked up the front staircase to the hotel.

The Biltmore was a perfect example of Los Angeles' delightful madness. It combined Italian, Spanish and, absurdly, French styles into an ornate orgy of frescos, caste bronze staircases, Mediterranean murals, and Romanesque columns. It probably caused epileptic seizures in traditional architects. And Elizabeth loved it.

An enormous double grand staircase led to a bank of elevators, but instead of going up, Alan led them down a staircase into a cavernous posh nightclub. The Sala D'Oro was filled to capacity. Dozens and dozens of tables, with white linen and silver and candles made a crescent around the dance floor. In front of the stage an entire orchestra sat playing Cole Porter standards.

They'd barely reached the bottom of the stairs before Alan began shaking hands and gliding from table to table as he made his way across the room. He always introduced them as "my dear friends, Simon and Elizabeth Cross" as though they'd known each other for years and not hours.

As they approached yet another table, Elizabeth noticed Simon staring at something across the room. She followed his eye line and saw one of the men from Musso & Frank. He sat at a table with several other men she didn't recognize.

"Elizabeth," Alan said, touching her arm to get her attention.

Elizabeth turned around and there was no mistaking the woman at Alan's side. Even without the introduction, Elizabeth knew who she was. Her platinum blonde hair and bombshell figure gave her away. Jean Harlow. She was Marilyn before there was a Marilyn.

"How'd ya do?" she said, flashing a grin. "Any friend of Alan's and all that."

She was so beautiful and vivacious; it was hard to believe she'd pass away just a few years later. Even better than meeting her was seeing Simon's expression as he turned to shake her hand. Whatever or whoever he'd been expecting it wasn't Jean Harlow. His eyes widened in a wonderfully cartoony way. He licked his lips twice before stammering a smitten hello and casting Elizabeth a nervous glance. Didn't watch old movies, my eye, Elizabeth thought.

"See you at Eastside?" Jean asked Alan.

"Wouldn't miss it."

Jean blew them all a kiss and disappeared into the crowd. Alan held out a chair for Elizabeth at the vacated table. As Simon sat down next to her she whispered, "Just Monty Python?"

Simon tugged on his collar as a bright red blush crawled up his neck.

"Are you blushing?" she asked. It was adorable.

Try as he might, Simon couldn't conjure a scowl and pretended to busy himself with adjusting the perfectly perfect cuff of his shirt.

Alan caught a waiter's eye and gestured to the table.

"That man from Musso & Frank is here, who is he?" Elizabeth asked trying to sound casual.

"The cigar with a man stuck to it? That, my darling, is Sam Roth—the head of Mammoth Studios and my most gracious employer. Sam!" Alan raised one of the abandoned glasses on the table in mock salute. "You colossal pain in my ass," Alan added under his breath.

Sam Roth grunted, not that he could hear what Alan said, and turned back to his friends.

Alan put the glass down and sighed. "Where is that waiter?"

For the next half hour, Simon and Elizabeth nursed their drinks and tried to get a little more information out of Alan, but an endless stream of people coming to the table constantly interrupted them. Elizabeth was trying again when a busty redhead appeared behind Alan and tapped him on the shoulder.

No sooner had he turned around in his chair than she threw a drink in his face.

Alan wiped the water away calmly and stood. "Viv—"

"Don't you Viv me, I've been waitin' six weeks for you to call," she said in a brassy voice with an intermittent east coast accent.

"Viv." Alan tried to take her hand, but she yanked it away. "I'm sorry."

"Sorry?" she said loudly. "What does that mean?"

"I never meant to hurt you, my dear. You must believe—"

The ringing sound of the slap caused the tables nearby to fall into stunned and eager silence. Elizabeth and Simon, both on high alert now, started to rise out of their seats, but without even looking their way, Alan lifted a hand to stop them.

Alan stood his ground calmly and accepted her anger.

Vivian's pique had burned itself out and now she looked around at the staring faces. She threw back her head with as much triumph as she could muster and marched off. Alan kept his place until she was several tables away. Moments later the conversation around them hummed back to life.

Alan sat back down at the table. His joie de vivre tinged with a sad sort of thoughtfulness. He noticed the unasked question in Elizabeth's eyes. Why had he just stood there and taken that?

"She deserved her moment." He smiled ruefully and took a deep swig from his teacup. "Everyone should have at least one."

Elizabeth wanted to hug him, but settled for something else. "Mr. Grant? Would you dance with me?"

Alan smiled, buoyed back to life, and was about to accept when he remembered his manners. "Do you mind?" he asked Simon.

"No, of course not."

Alan stood and held out his hand for Elizabeth.

"Just don't let her lead," Simon said as they started toward the crowded dance floor.

Elizabeth just had time to turn back and stick out her tongue at Simon before Alan spun her around and took her into his arms.

The dance floor was so crowded all anyone could really do was sway. Alan Grant did even that with style. Despite it being packed with people, he managed to move them around the floor gracefully. Most of the couples around them were in formal dress—tuxedos and long gowns. There didn't seem to be any special event. Just going out on the town was the event in itself. Modern life seemed a bit flat by comparison.

"So," Alan said as he spun them out of the way of a man who'd had far too much tea and whose dancing was more like stumbling. "Who are you really?"

Elizabeth tensed and nearly stepped on his toes. "What do you mean?"

"Do you work for him?" Alan asked as lightly and casually as if he were asking if she'd read any good books lately.

"Work for who?"

Alan looked down at her, into her eyes, and gone was the drunken playboy. His blue eyes bore into her, sharp and keen, just for a moment before they softened again. "No. Not you," he said, maneuvering them deftly across the floor. "Perhaps you're an angel sent to help me. Yes, I think that is who you are."

"Do you need an angel?"

Alan pulled her closer. "Doesn't everyone?"

SIMON WATCHED ELIZABETH AND Grant drift in and out of the crowd on the dance floor. Hopefully, she was learning something. It was damned maddening not to have any idea what they were up against. Was there some sort of supernatural creature after him? Was it a woman scorned? Judging from earlier, that was a definite possibility. How could they possibly protect Grant from something they couldn't see coming?

Simon studied the people around him. None of them seemed particularly out of the ordinary, except for Sam Roth. Sitting just a table away, Simon could hear most of the conversation. So far, it amounted to nothing more than talk of the studio's business affairs, which were surprisingly good. Considering the Great Depression was already four years old, most businesses were struggling, and many were already dead. From the exchanges Simon overheard, Mammoth Studios was doing much better than most.

Simon turned his attention back to the dance floor. He was uncomfortable with having either of them out of his sight for too long. Unknown danger and Elizabeth attracted each other and were a rather potent mixture. The orchestra bridged from the slow standards to a fast-paced jitterbug and the dance floor changed from swaying wheat to pennies on a drum.

"You gotta help me."

The woman's voice came from Sam Roth's table and it was so close Simon thought she was talking to him. He turned around, but quickly realized she was talking to Roth. It was the girl from Musso & Frank and she'd been crying a great deal, from the state of her make-up.

"Calm down, Ruby." Roth was not happy to see her, but it was clear he couldn't get rid of her without a scene. She was in a state of near panic. Her fingers worked the edges of the tablecloth and her breath came in short, quick gasps punctuated with tearful sniffles.

"Give us the table?" Roth asked the three men sitting with him. Not one of the three hesitated to leave as quickly as possible.

Simon pretended to be watching the dancers and listening to the music. He tapped his fork gently against the tablecloth in time to the rhythm and searched again for Elizabeth on the dance floor.

Once the other men were gone, Ruby moved her chair closer to Roth's.

"Benny here too?" Sam Roth asked looking over her shoulder.

Ruby shook her head. "He's at the Star," she said breathlessly between sniffles. "He said you wouldn't help, but I said he was wrong."

Roth took off his glasses and polished the thin round lenses with a napkin. "I've already told you," he said in a hushed voice. "There's nothing I can do."

"There's gotta be something. I'll work for free, for the rest of my life." Ruby clutched at his jacket sleeve. "I'll do anything."

"That's what got you in this mess," Roth bit out angrily. "This isn't my doing."

"You introduced us," she said a bit too loudly and then looked around to see if anyone had heard.

Simon shifted in his seat, turning his back slightly to their table and checked his watch.

Roth put his glasses back on and tossed the napkin on the table.

"I didn't know. I didn't think it was real. It was stupid," Ruby said quickly and quietly, the words tumbling out in desperation. She could see her pleas were having no effect and tried something new. "What about your brother? Or Grant? If you can help them, maybe you can help me."

Roth's anger and frustration grew. "I can't," he said more loudly than he'd meant to. He picked up the stub of his cigar and shook his head. "You and Benny and the others, you did this to yourselves."

"But, we only have a few days—"

"There's nothing I can do." There was a cold finality to the words and to Sam Roth.

Ruby let go of Roth's jacket sleeve and fought back a fresh wave of tears. She smoothed the tablecloth and nodded, resigned. "Yeah."

Sam cast a quick look at her, shoved the cigar into his mouth and needlessly pushed away his water glass.

"Yeah," Ruby repeated as she stood. She paused and looked down at Sam Roth, her panic now more resignation than anything. "I just wanted to be somebody."

In a daze, Ruby walked away from Roth's table. After a moment, Roth looked after her. He crushed the dying ember of his cigar into the large glass ashtray at the center of the table and gestured to someone across the room.

A big man in a suit one size too small for his muscles appeared almost instantly at Roth's side. "Yes, Mr. Roth?"

"Let's get the hell out of here."

Whatever Grant was mixed up in, these others were too, and, apparently, the clock was ticking.

Shortly after Roth left, Elizabeth and Grant reappeared at the table. Her cheeks were flushed from dancing and she was slightly out of breath.

"Phew," she said reaching for a glass of water. "That's hot work."

"And thirsty work," Alan added, draining what was left in his teacup "I know a little place…"

Grant must have a hollow leg. Or two. Simon had never seen anyone drink so much and remain conscious.

Elizabeth puffed out a breath. "I don't know."

"Where is your sense of adventure?" He took her hand and started to slowly lead her away. "Come away with me, Lucia, across the seven seas…"

Elizabeth gave Simon a helpless look and then called over her shoulder. "Don't forget my purse."

Simon grunted and rolled his eyes. He found her small purse under a discarded linen napkin. Simon sighed, tucked the clutch into his pocket and followed them into the crowd. By the time he turned back around, he'd nearly lost sight of them. This was going to be one of those nights.

THEIR NEXT PORT OF call was hidden in one of the many wooded canyons surrounding Los Angeles—an old fashioned speakeasy. Elizabeth knew them well. She and Simon had spent weeks working in one in New York. This club was definitely more upscale, but the clientele was just as drunk.

Alan was greeted by the owner, a squat little man with three long wisps of hair that curled around the top of his bald head in a valiant effort to cover it. He was bright-eyed with excitement to see a star of Grant's caliber in his little place. As he ushered them to an empty table, the usual murmur from star-struck patrons followed them. They took their seats and the owner brought them a round of brown plaid, which turned out to be Scotch. Sort of.

Simon sniffed his glass and set it down untouched. Elizabeth let her curiosity get the better of her and took a small sip. It made her eyes burn and her ears tingle.

"Charming place, isn't it?" Alan said, drinking his as though it were from the top shelf and not the bathtub out back.

"Delightful," Simon said, pushing his drink further away.

Simon could be a killjoy if he wanted to, but Elizabeth loved it. It was exciting and lively and…

"You stink! You hear me, Grant?"

A heavyset man across the room tipped back his chair until it was precariously balanced against the wall and stuck out a meaty finger in Alan's direction. "Youuu stink!" He chuckled to himself and his three friends at the table urged him on.

Alan ignored him. "Don't let it bother you," he said to Elizabeth, seeing her glare.

The man struggled to stand and only managed it when one of his friends, who was almost as pie-eyed as he was, helped. "That last movie you made…" he said holding his nose dramatically. He wobbled on unsteady legs and braced himself against the table. "It stunk."

Alan pretended not to hear or notice him. "Have you been to the Jungle Room yet? Wonderful band."

"Grant!" the man called out again.

Elizabeth shifted uncomfortably in her chair and tried to ignore him. "No, we haven't yet."

"There's a delightful Cuban restaurant nearby—"

"The worst one," the drunk said loudly, "was that damn pirate movie."

Elizabeth turned in her chair and the words were out before she could stop them. "You don't know what you're taking about. *Sword of the Seven Seas* was a classic."

"Elizabeth," Simon warned under his breath.

"Well, it is," she said under her breath as she turned back to their table.

Alan shook his head. "Best to ignore them," he said and then lifted his drink to his mouth, a small smile curving his lips. "A classic? Really?"

The drunken man shoved off from his table and stumbled toward them. Elizabeth felt Simon tense next to her. This could go boobies up pretty quickly she realized.

The man stopped a few feet away and bent awkwardly at the waist, leaning precariously forward. "You sound like my wife," he said jabbing a finger toward her. "Figures. You dumb broads always stick together, don't ya?"

Even from a few feet away, his breath was a toxic cloud that made Elizabeth cough. The crowd near them fell silent.

"She had a big fat mouth she couldn't keep shut," the man belched. "Just like you."

"That's enough." Simon pushed his chair back and stood menacingly next to her.

The man straightened up and pushed his shoulders back. He wobbled on unsteady legs and looked at Simon through bloodshot eyes. He squinted and wrinkled his nose.

"Go back to your table," Simon said calmly, but Elizabeth could see from the slight flexing of his fingers, the line of his jaw and the timbre of his voice, he was far from calm.

Alan lit a cigarette, content for now to watch from the sidelines.

Elizabeth knew she had to do something to diffuse the situation and stood up between the two men. "There's no reason to—"

"Shuddup," the drunk said and grabbed Elizabeth's arm, pulling her roughly to the side. "Gonna teach you a lesson—"

In two quick strides, Simon was around the table and wrenching Elizabeth out of the man's grasp. He grabbed a fist full of the man's shirt so quickly, his other hand barely had time to form a fist before it collided with the man's jaw.

The drunken man stumbled back from the force of the blow and collided with a nearby table, sending drinks skittering to the floor. He staggered back a few more steps and landed neatly in the chair he'd just vacated. The crowd erupted into spontaneous applause.

"Well done, Cross!" Alan said. "Hole in one!"

Simon grimaced and shook out his hand before turning to glare down at Elizabeth.

She shrugged sheepishly. "Well, it is a classic."

Simon was apparently not amused. "Are you all right?"

Before she could answer, Alan cleared his throat and nodded toward the man's table. He'd roused enough to stand again and wasn't alone this time. His three friends stood next to him and all four looked loaded for bear.

Everyone at the nearby tables scrambled to safety. The entirety of the bar had parted like the red sea leaving the two groups standing off and with no easy way to escape.

Alan sighed, downed his scotch and stood next to Simon. "Dicey odds. Four against two."

"Three," Elizabeth said trying to squeeze between them.

"Elizabeth," Simon hissed over his shoulder. "Would you please—"

"Look out!" she cried.

He turned just in time to sidestep a vicious rabbit punch from the first of the four. Simon replied with a quick, short jab to the man's ribs and an uppercut Liston would have envied. The man fell back against his friend, the big one who'd started it, who shoved his buddy out of the way. He raised a meaty fist and Elizabeth threw what was left of her scotch in his face temporarily blinding him. The few seconds it bought was enough time for Simon to land a right cross.

Elizabeth turned just in time to see Alan gracefully duck under a wild, drunken swing from one of the men. The man stumbled forward and Alan picked up his wooden chair and shattered it against the man's back. He fell onto their table and it collapsed under his weight with a thundering crash. Alan grinned proudly at his handiwork and never saw the man come at him from behind. The two of them went down in a pile landing on top of the unconscious man.

Elizabeth leaned over them and tried to pull the man off Alan. She yanked at his collar, but couldn't get him to budge. She heard the sound of a fist hitting flesh. It wasn't like the movies at all. There was no sharp crack or kapow; it was just a dull, sickening thud. That's when she saw Simon fly past her and slide across the floor. He finally came to a stop and pushed himself up on his elbow. He blinked, trying to regain his senses and worked his jaw. There was a small trickle of blood coming from his lip. The man she'd left him fighting, the one who'd heckled Alan, lumbered across the room toward him. She did the only thing she could think of and ran toward him.

She leapt up and landed on his back like a crazed monkey. He swung around and she nearly flew off, but held on for dear life. Her arms wound around his neck and her legs tried to grip his waist, but he was too big around. Her fingers worked their way up his face, gouging and poking whatever they touched. He clawed at her hands and finally gripped her arm so tightly she thought it might break.

He grunted and pried her off his back. With surprising ease, he tossed her aside. She flew through the air. It was an odd slow motion sensation and she had just enough time to realize her underwear was showing as she braced herself for the floor that rushed up to meet her. Instead of smashing into the concrete, she collided with something else. Or was it someone else? It took a second to register what had happened. She hadn't hit the ground; someone had caught her. She felt strong arms hold her just a bit more tightly. She opened her eyes to see Alan smiling down at her. "Hello."

He set her down and she saw the man Alan had been fighting curled up in a ball. His hands cradled his man parts, his friend unconscious on the floor next to him. She looked at Alan, who merely shrugged.

She turned to find Simon and started to rush to his side, but Alan held her arm. "Let him have the honors."

Seeing Elizabeth tossed like a ragdoll seemed to have been all Simon had needed to clear his head. The drunken man stumbled on legs of jelly in front him. Simon stood and delivered a quick combination, punctuated with a gut punch Elizabeth felt across the room. The man doubled over onto the floor, clutching his stomach. Simon took a step closer to him and loomed over him. Simon's chest heaved from his efforts.

He wiped the blood from his chin with the back of his hand. "Lesson over."

Elizabeth hurried over to Simon's side.

"Bravo," Alan said.

THE THREE GOT OUT while the going was good and Peter drove them down the winding mountain roads. Elizabeth made sure Simon was all right, and thankfully, except for a few bruises, he was. Grant drank some more and recounted his favorite moments of the evening as they drove home. Slowly, the liquor and gentle ride of the car lulled him to sleep and he slumped down in his seat, a dreamy smile on his face.

Elizabeth sighed and snuggled into Simon's side. She laid her head on his shoulder and rested a hand on his chest. "We're no closer than we were when the night started."

Simon was drifting off himself and it took a moment for her words to register. "Hmm?"

"To finding out what sort of danger he's in," Elizabeth clarified, nodding toward a sleeping Alan Grant.

"Yes, well, other than going to bars with you…"

Elizabeth lifted her head off his shoulder. "Sorry 'bout that."

Simon shook his head and pulled her closer. "It wasn't your fault."

She laid her head back on his shoulder.

"Entirely," he finished.

Elizabeth laughed softly. "I am sorry. Last time we almost lost—" She sat up suddenly. "The watch?"

If they'd lost it in the fight…

Simon plunged his hand into his jacket pocket and huffed out a relieved breath. "Safe."

Thank god for that. Elizabeth leaned her head back against Simon's shoulder and they rode in silence through the nearly desolate streets of early morning Los Angeles.

Grant's home was a gated mansion in the heart of Beverly Hills. Simon and Elizabeth waited downstairs in the immense foyer while Peter helped Grant up the grand staircase.

When they reached the top of the stairs, Grant stopped and turned around dramatically. "Now cracks a noble heart. Goodnight sweet prince…ess, and flights of angels sing me to my rest."

With that Peter and Grant disappeared on the landing above.

"I wish we knew how to help him," Elizabeth said still staring at the top of the empty staircase before turning to Simon.

Simon nodded thoughtfully. "Did you learn anything when you were dancing? Did he say anything that might give us a hint?"

"Not really. Just that he is in trouble," she said looking back up at the top of the empty stairs. "Something big too. I'm worried."

Simon tucked a stray hair behind Elizabeth's ear and caressed her cheek. "Honestly, I'm not sure what I learned either. And I'm too knackered to think about it."

Elizabeth captured Simon's hand and gently kissed his abraded knuckles. "Does it hurt much?"

He shook his head. She leaned in close. "And this?" His split lip wasn't too swollen, but it must still hurt. She pushed herself up and kissed the corner of his mouth tenderly.

"Elizabeth," he said in a voice that was soft and rough at the same time.

Above them, a door closed and footsteps started toward the stairs. Elizabeth started to move in for another kiss when she got an idea and pulled away from a confused Simon. She frantically scanned the room and then shoved her purse under the edge of a massive flower arrangement on a nearby table.

"What on earth are you doing?" Simon asked.

"Giving us a reason to come back."

Before Simon could respond, Peter came down the stairs and apologized for keeping them waiting.

"Is he all right?" Elizabeth asked.

"He'll be fine, miss. Back to himself in the morning. Now," Peter said, putting his chauffeur's cap back on, "where can I take you?"

DOWN. THAT'S WHERE SHE would be going. Down, down, down.

Ruby tried to be quiet, but the brush under her feet cracked like brittle bones. She knew the man in the shack was a heavy sleeper. She'd been to the Hollywoodland sign before. But it had been so different then. Everything had been so different then. She'd come here with a boy, to be on the top of the world, and now she was looking for the bottom.

She could see the glow from the letters behind the bushes ahead. In her haste, in her fear, she tripped on an exposed root and tumbled to the ground. Rocks and twigs scraped her palms and her knees, but she didn't care. It didn't matter. None of it mattered. She was stupid. The same stupid little girl who'd left Cedar Falls and believed the lies. This whole damned thing was a lie.

Ruby pushed herself back up and emerged from the bushes. The lights were nearly blinding. She forced her eyes open and let them burn.

The first letter was closest. End at the beginning. That was how it should be. Her hands shook as she grabbed the bottom rung of the ladder, but she kept on. She'd failed at everything else she'd tried. She would not fail at this. Rung after rung, she climbed higher and higher. The heat from the lights made her hands sweat. She nearly slipped once, but held on. She laughed at the irony.

She didn't know how long it took. It didn't matter. Finally, she reached the top and the city below looked like the fairyland she'd always dreamed it was. Lights flickered in the distance, full of promise, full of evil.

For a moment, Ruby froze. Hope flared in her chest. She wanted to live. She wanted to take it all back. She could just see her brother's face. Poor Walter. She would have done anything in that instant to take it back. And with that thought, the flicker of hope died. There was no escape. She thought she was so clever, but she was the same stupid little girl she'd always been. She deserved what was to come.

Suddenly, she couldn't move fast enough. Her foot slipped on the rung as she edged to the very top. She balanced on the edge, the lights below shining up at her, worshipping her one last time.

And then she jumped.

CHAPTER SEVEN

FDR KEPT STARING AT him. It was disconcerting. Jack stared back, but it didn't do any good. Finally, he did what he should have done in the first place and flipped the Life magazine over. With a bored sigh, Jack went back to reading about "how Lupe Valez gets her man" in the latest issue of Hollywood magazine. Again.

He'd tried to follow the man from Musso & Frank last night, but the man just disappeared on him. Not that he would have gotten too far on foot anyway. By the time he'd circled back to the restaurant, Simon and Elizabeth were already gone.

Jack made a few inquiries, but people were pretty tight-lipped and he didn't have enough grease in his pocket to loosen them up. He'd recognized Sam Roth from Mammoth Studios and the girl, Ruby, he'd seen her in a few pictures. He'd never seen Roth's brother, but he'd heard about him before. With that mug, he had to Benny Roth.

Jack tried to bide his time until he was supposed to check in, but if he was honest with himself he was worried, and hungry. It was a bad combination.

The house of cards he'd started building at seven that morning lay flat on the coffee table, having been besieged by an onslaught of flicked peanuts. The shells littered the edges of the table.

Jack's stomach growled. Just the thought of food made him hungry. He'd eaten most of the ammunition after the house fell, but he saw one that got away tucked under the edge of the side table. He picked up the linty peanut and blew off the bit of fluff before popping it into his mouth. What he wouldn't give for a short-stack of buttermilk pancakes from The Pantry or a big plate of steak and eggs from Clifton's. Elizabeth would love that place.

Jack tossed aside Lupe Valez and hoisted himself off the sofa and checked his watch, again. It was early, but he didn't care. He picked up the phone and tapped the cradle. The hotel switchboard operator put through the call to the Ambassador.

"Cross?" Jack said, more relieved than he wanted to admit to hear Simon's voice. "You two all right?"

Simon assured him they were fine and brought Jack up to speed on what little they'd learned last night at the Biltmore.

"Sam Roth's a tough old bastard, but a straight shooter, I think. His brother, Benny though, keep an eye on that one. He's pretty well connected."

"Connected, as in the mob?" Simon asked.

"Sort of. He's heavy into bootlegging and the rackets. I remember some buddies telling me stories about Benny Roth. Not pretty. He's got some powerful friends too. Be careful with him." Jack scratched his stubbly chin. "Maybe I should do a little digging, see if I can find out what he's caught up in."

Simon was silent on the other end of the line. Jack could almost hear Simon thinking. "You'll be discreet?"

Jack grinned. "Like seamless underwear."

"Wells—"

"I did this for a living, remember?"

There was another pause before Simon spoke again. "All right. After breakfast, we're going back to Grant's. We'll be out most of the day, but I'll call back for messages. If you find anything, call us."

"I'll check in with you by six, all right?"

"Agreed."

Jack pulled his jacket from the back of a nearby chair and slipped it on while he talked. "And be careful. I don't know Grant or what he's mixed up in, but if Benny Roth's involved, you can bet it's shady."

"I understand."

"Give Elizabeth a big kiss for me."

"Wells—"

"Just lay one right on her—"

SIMON HUNG UP THE phone and glared at it. Not that he was genuinely angry; he knew Wells was just having a go at him. Despite Simon's misgivings about bringing him with them to 1933, he trusted Jack. He'd proven to be a valuable ally in England and, much to Simon's surprise, a good friend to them both when they returned home to California. It was a bit chancy to let him wander around the city, but if what they faced here was remotely as dangerous as the things they'd faced before, having Jack work with them was well worth the risk.

Simon moved the phone to the far side of the table and flexed his bruised knuckles. He felt a far sight better than he'd imagined he would. Elizabeth had apologized for most of the night. The memory brought a smile to his lips.

He shook the memory away and reached for a silver cloche-covered plate from the room service tray. While Elizabeth slept in, which she excelled at and after last night no doubt needed, Simon was, as usual, up early. He'd walked the grounds before coming back to the bungalow and ordering breakfast. The Ambassador's service was first class. The waiter had laid the table on the south patio with care. White linens, silver and fine china waited on the polished glass table just out of the morning sun.

Simon sipped his tea and considered what lay ahead. They'd learned precious little last night during their frolic with Alan Grant. He was clearly in some sort of trouble and either or both Roth brothers were involved. Where the other man or the girl, Ruby, fit in, Simon wasn't sure, but her desperation was troubling.

Simon pushed out a long, frustrated breath and lifted the cover to his plate. No use in letting it go cold.

"Not gonna wait for me?" Elizabeth said from the doorway behind him.

"I was wondering if you were ever—" The rest of the sentence and the thought melted away as he turned and saw her.

Elizabeth leaned against the doorway, wearing nothing but one of his oxford shirts. The hem fell just about mid-thigh and his eyes lingered there before working their way back up to her face, eyes still drowsy with sleep. The shirt was absurdly large for her and she'd done a poor job of rolling the sleeves up. So poor, in fact, that one sleeve was already unrolling itself. The hand she perched delicately on her hip in mock annoyance was swallowed by the fabric.

Simon felt the familiar rush of desire. Elizabeth always made him feel that way, but at her most unassuming the effect was stunning. It was, however, more than passion that coursed through his body at the sight of her. It was hope and faith and promise. It was everything good in the world infused in a single moment. It was having her as his wife.

Elizabeth offered him a sleepy smile, and pushed off from the doorway. "Good morning."

She leaned down to kiss him. Simon cupped her cheek, still warm from sleep. "Good morning, yourself."

Elizabeth took a seat at the table and rubbed her hands together in greedy anticipation. "Is this what I think it is?"

She took off the cloche and her smile answered her own question. "Eggs Benedict." She took in a deep, satisfied breath, enjoying the rich, delicate aroma of a perfect Hollandaise sauce, poured herself a cup of coffee and settled in to breakfast.

Simon shook open his linen napkin and laid it in his lap.

He filled her in on his conversation with Wells, emphasizing as Wells had, the potential for danger regarding Benny Roth and his mob connections.

Elizabeth washed down a bite of eggs with a sip of coffee. "Bootlegging isn't exactly a booming business anymore. I mean it won't be for long anyway. Prohibition's almost over. Beer's legal in a few days and the rest of it will be legal in a few months."

Even though Simon had spent nearly two months living through Prohibition when they'd traveled back in time to New York, he'd never given much thought to what it meant when the Amendment was repealed. Organized and not-so-organized crime had built an enormous and profitable industry that was going to cease to be in a few months. "That's a great deal of income that's not easily replaced. Might make a man desperate."

"You think he might be blackmailing the others for money? Alan or his brother?"

"That's possible," Simon conceded. "Wells wanted to look into it."

Elizabeth eagerly started to say something, probably along the lines of singing Wells' praises, but quickly schooled her expression.

Simon popped a piece of toast into his mouth. "Despite his sometimes," Simon said searching for the right words, "excessive charm, he is a good man and good at what he does. I fear that before this is over, we will need all the help we can get."

Elizabeth nodded thoughtfully. "Alan's definitely in trouble. I hope we can get him to trust us."

"I have faith." Simon said as he tossed aside his napkin.

"You do?"

"In you."

JACK DIDN'T USUALLY DRINK before noon, but people didn't exactly go to Jilly's for the ambiance. The place stunk of stale beer and even staler people. Even compared to other speakeasies, Jilly's was a pit. It used to be one of Benny Roth's best joints, a place to get a cold beer and warm girl. Now, all that was left were the dregs—faded pictures over the bar, peeling wallpaper stained with too much cigarette smoke and a clientele one step up from the drink tank.

Jack hunched over his drink and recreated in his mind's eye what and who was around him. It was an old habit and a damn good one for a spy to have—he'd memorized the room as soon as he walked in. He stared down into his drink and replayed what he remembered.

A man gently snored face down at a table behind him. His arm was wrapped around his beer glass like a child holding his teddy bear, and a racing tip sheet stuck out of his front right jacket pocket. Another sat at the far end of the bar, unshaven, unwashed and staring blankly at the dingy mirror beneath a faded picture of Lillian Gish. Flat soulless eyes stared back in his reflection. Jack had seen that look often enough. Too often. First in the Depression and then in the war. It was a man who'd been carved out. Life had scraped away any last bit of hope and all that was left was a shell.

Jack sipped his whisky and let the burn of it as it trickled down his throat remind him he wasn't one of them. He was playing a part. Just a part. No one paid attention to a drunk, especially one who was already liquored up before lunch. Jack mumbled to himself and scratched his stubbled cheek.

He'd heard that Benny Roth made the rounds each day at about noon. Check on the till, throw his muscle around, make sure people knew his face. Benny liked to be in the spotlight. But in this hole it was pretty dim.

Right on cue, the bright California sunshine raced into the room through the open door and ran away as it shut. It took Jack's eyes a minute to adjust from the flash of light. Two men had entered. One with muscles for brains and the other was Benny Roth. He swore under his breath as he looked around the bar.

"Waste of damn time," Roth said to no one in particular. He yanked a chair back from a table and brushed away the dust and crumbs with his hat before sitting down.

The bartender, a flat-nosed man who reeked of cheap cigars and camphor oil, nodded and ducked into a back room. Roth's bodyguard took up sentry position at the door. Jack could feel his eyes boring into him. The last thing he needed was trouble. His stomach rumbled. The eggs he'd had for breakfast must had been as old as the waitress who'd served them. The bodyguard kept staring and Jack met his gaze with a confused squint, and then offered the idiot a sloppy smile and a loud burp. It seemed to do the trick and the bodyguard turned his attention elsewhere.

The bartender came back into the room and handed Roth a sheet of paper. Jack could smell the fresh glass of whisky on the man's breath across the room. The man rubbed the back of his sweaty neck and waited nervously. Whatever he'd handed Roth, it wasn't good news.

"Pathetic," Roth said when he'd finished reading. "I thought we'd at least get a few more months out of it."

"Yeah, well," the bartender said, "beer's always been our best seller and—"

Roth slowly turned in his chair and looked up at the man whose voice trailed off helplessly.

"You think I'm stupid?" Roth said.

"No!"

"You think I don't know what tomorrow means?" The man started to protest, to try to dig himself out of the hole he'd dug, but Roth didn't give him the chance. "Get out of my sight."

The man hurried behind the bar and busied himself with polishing a stack of dirty glasses. Roth took out a silver cigarette lighter and set fire to the piece of paper. He held it in the air in front of him as the flames grew. The light from the small fire danced in his eyes.

The front door opened and two men filled the doorway. The silhouettes gave them away in an instant. Broad shouldered and fat bellied. They wore round-brimmed military caps and an air of confidence well beyond cocky. The light from the small fire danced on the gold of the shields pinned to their chests.

"Takin' up arson, now are ya, Benji?" one of them said as he took off his cap and tucked it under his arm. His face was ruddy and pockmarked with dozens of deep scars. It left him looking half-made of clay and half-made of man.

Benny Roth made a sour face and forced a laugh as he let the paper fall to the floor and crushed out the remaining flames with the heel of his shoe. "Are you offering lessons, McCray?"

McCray's beetle black eyes flashed at that and his partner shot him an anxious look. McCray shrugged it away with a casual wave of his hand and a thin smile. The two men joined Roth at the little table.

McCray looked around the bar. His eyes fell on Jack. A small jerk of the cop's head was the only message Jack needed. Without a word, he followed the unspoken order and took his drink to the far side of the bar. Keeping his gaze down, he sat down heavily in a chair against the wall and wiped his nose with the back of his hand.

He swallowed down the bile that rose in the back of his throat. God, he hated crooked cops. He'd grown up with them in Chicago and, dope that he was, he thought things would be different out here. But it was just more of the same. There were more crooked cops than palm trees in LA. They hooked their badges into every criminal enterprise in the city, even ran their own rackets.

Jack slumped against the wall and waited. If he knew anything about them, they were arrogant enough to talk openly. After all, what could anyone do? Call the cops?

Satisfied, McCray put his hat on the empty chair next him and spread his hands out. "So. We're here."

"We're wastin' our time, Willie," his partner said, leaning in conspiratorially, but speaking loud enough for everyone in the bar to hear. "This place is a dump."

"Shuddup," McCray said. The impatience and scorn in his voice brought his partner up short. McCray glared at him so long the other cop visibly flinched and then nervously started pulling on his fingers. Finally, McCray barked out a laugh and clapped his partner on the shoulder. "Butch has got a big mouth, but Roth, I gotta say, he's right. This place ain't up to scratch. The Shooting Star Club, maybe, but this…you know, we got standards."

"You gotta use your imagination," Roth said. "Good sized back room, second floor lookout, a little paint. Look like a million bucks. But the real value, you know, it's what I bring."

"Oh, so we need you. Here I thought it was the other way around."

McCray's partner laughed.

Roth chewed the inside of his cheek before replying. "I did good business for seven years. I built up a name and I got connections."

"He's got connections," McCray said to his partner in a voice full of false praise and then his voice was flat and cold as he turned back to Roth. "You got nothin'."

Roth sneered. "You call Mammoth nothing?"

McCray leaned back in his chair. "Oh, Mammoth's somethin', but, uhm, you're the wrong Roth. Unless somethin's changed, big brother holds those strings."

"Today he does."

"That's a hot potato," McCray said shaking his head.

"You leave my brother to me," Roth said. "He'll come around. One way or the other."

Chapter Eight

A LAN GRANT'S BEVERLY HILLS mansion was even more impressive in the daylight. Elizabeth walked toward the large, iron gate complete with the Charles Foster Kane cursive "AG" set in the middle while Simon paid the cabbie. She wrapped her hands around the cool metal and pressed her face between the bars for a better view. Last night, she'd been too tired and a little too tipsy to take it all in.

It was as if someone had taken a large Southern plantation and plopped it down in the middle of Beverly Hills. At the end of the long drive and beyond the weeping willows and tall oaks, the broad elegant façade of the antebellum South looked back. It was odd and out of place and yet, made perfect sense. It was one of the things she'd always loved about California and Los Angeles especially, the diversity.

She heard what sounded like a goose honking in the distance and pushed her head harder against the bars to try to see around the side of the hedge.

"Were you planning on squeezing through?" Simon said from behind her. His hand rested on an intercom box a few feet away. "Or should I buzz?"

Elizabeth pulled her head out from between the bars and gestured for him to go ahead. "I could have fit though," she said under her breath.

After Simon explained to Peter who they were, the gate made a clicking sound and then silently swung open. Elizabeth reached for Simon's hand. He gave a quick, reassuring smile, and then kissed the back of her hand. Together, they walked up the gravel drive toward Alan's house.

Peter had barely opened the door to let them in when they heard Alan's voice call out for him. For his part, Peter just sighed and shook his head. He stepped aside and pointed toward a small round table at the center of the foyer. "Your purse is over there, Miss."

"Peeeter!" Alan's voice echoed down the hall.

"Can we see him?" Elizabeth asked. "I'd like to make sure he's all right. After last night..."

"I'm sure he'd like that," Peter said. "This way." He led them down a long marble-tiled hallway to a back door. He opened it for them and gestured for them to precede him. They stepped out onto a small landing that overlooked the pool.

It was beautiful. The pool was a large glassy rectangle rimmed with curved white marble edges. A long building sat at the far edge with billowing curtains caught in the breeze giving glimpses inside each cabana. A grand open room sat between them filled with brightly colored pillows and long plush divans.

"You have guests, Mr. Grant," Peter called as he joined them and led them down the small staircase and into the pool area.

Alan lay stretched out on his back on a poolside chaise, fully dressed in a light cotton suit, his Panama hat resting atop his face, and what was left of a Bloody Mary dangling precariously from the fingers of his left hand. "Who is it?" he asked tiredly from beneath his hat.

"Hello," Elizabeth said.

"Lucia," Alan said and she could hear the smile in his voice. He barked out a delighted laugh, pulled his hat to rest on his stomach and lifted himself up onto an elbow. "My angel returns."

It was Simon's turn to laugh. "Angel? Wait until you spend a little more time with her."

Alan grinned and swung his legs to the ground. "Cross. You look well. Recovered from our adventure?" He seemed genuinely pleased to see them.

Simon rubbed his jaw. "For the most part."

"Sit, sit, please." He held up his nearly empty glass. "Drink? Peter!"

Peter, who had remained in the background, stepped forward. "Sir?"

"There you are," Alan said. "I get the distinct feeling you've been avoiding me this morning. Or is it my imagination?"

"That could be, sir," Peter replied enigmatically. He pulled up a chair for Elizabeth before doing the same for Simon.

Alan frowned. "Is there some reason or does it simply amuse you?"

Peter stepped forward. "I didn't want you to see this." He pulled a folded newspaper out of his jacket pocket.

Alan squinted at it before waving him closer. "You know I don't care what they say."

Reluctantly, Peter handed him the newspaper, Variety, the Hollywood trade magazine. "It's not a review, sir."

"Well, what—" Alan started as he unfolded the paper. "Damn." He closed his eyes tightly for a long moment before looking at the headline again and skimming the story. "Damn, damn, *damn*."

When he looked up from the paper, his eyes were full of unshed tears and a deep bone-weary sadness. There was something helpless and wounded and even a little afraid in him. Elizabeth's heart ached. She reached out instinctively and touched his arm.

Alan sat up a bit straighter. "One of the," he started and then cleared his throat. "One of the darker sides of the dream, I'm afraid." He handed Simon the paper.

The headline read: Starlet Takes Her Final Bow…Off Hollywoodland Sign. "This is the girl from last night," Simon said pointing at the small round inset image next to the story of a young starlet who leapt to her death from the Hollywoodland sign. "Ruby."

"Yes." Alan drank down the last bits of his drink, stared into the empty glass and set it aside. "Such a pity."

He was trying, and failing, to sound like anyone who'd heard of the untimely death of a stranger. It was clear to Elizabeth, even if she hadn't seen them at Musso & Frank last night that he held some attachment to the girl. "Were you," she started cautiously, "involved?"

Alan's eyes snapped to hers. "No," he said fervently and then repeated more softly. "No. She was just a child."

"But you knew her," Elizabeth pressed. "She was at your table last night."

"She was at the Biltmore as well," Simon said. "She pleaded with Sam Roth for help."

"Did she?" Alan asked, sounding unsurprised by the news.

"She was desperate." Simon folded the paper. "I didn't realize how much."

"There was nothing you could do," Alan said, not unkindly. He stared down at the ground and then massaged the inside of his elbow as if it ached. "Nothing anyone can do."

The shift in tense wasn't lost on either Simon or Elizabeth, and they exchanged a quick, concerned glance. He sounded so forlorn, so defeated; Elizabeth got out of her chair and knelt in front of him. She took both of his hands into hers. "Maybe we can help."

When Alan looked up at her, she thought for a moment he was going to confide his secrets. His water blue eyes glittered with emotion and then a smile quirked his lips. "It is beyond even the realm of angels," he whispered. He patted her hands and his emotions shifted like waves sloshing in a pool.

"Now," he said, his voice firm and filled with his natural, mischievous spark of life. "About that drink…"

JACK SQUINTED UP AT the midday sun. It felt good to be out of Jilly's and in the light of day again. Once he'd gotten out, he'd just walked. Anything was better than being cooped up in his little hotbox of an apartment. He didn't need to check in with Simon and Elizabeth for hours yet.

It felt good to stretch his legs, but even back in the 1930's LA wasn't a walking town. Too spread out. So, he'd hopped on a Red Car in mid-city and headed west. He always seemed to be heading west.

He'd been damn lucky to overhear what he had, although he wasn't quite sure what to make of it. The cops hadn't stayed long, thankfully. McCray did give him one last lingering look before they left. He held it long enough for Jack to wonder if he'd been sniffed out, but in the end McCray and his partner left him alone and left Benny Roth to stew.

What was Roth up to? Was he blackmailing his brother for the studio? And if he was, where did the others fit in? Alan Grant worked for Mammoth. Maybe that was the connection? He looked up at the street signs. He wasn't far from the studio. Maybe he could do a little poking around. He headed down Washington Boulevard into Culver City, the real heart of Hollywood film production, unknown to the outside world. Little production bungalows and small Spanish-style houses that the studio workers lived in started to dot the rural landscape as he got closer to the enormous studio. He could see it just ahead—several city blocks walled off by non-descript cinderblocks on the outside. Inside, full street replicas of New York City, a little Spanish town, lakes and jungles and enough office buildings for a few thousand people. He'd gotten his job in Hollywood at Mammoth. He'd worked there a few times in the past or was it the future? Time travel was hell on tenses.

Larger buildings replaced the bungalows. Bodegas, restaurants, small hotels, shops, all sprung up around each studio like old-time, army camp followers. Where there were studios, there was money and jobs. Men of all ages, from young boys to old men, hung around the gates hoping for a crumb, for a job. Sometimes, they got lucky. He'd been one of the lucky ones.

When he'd left his family in Chicago, he had no idea where he was going or what he was going to do. He just knew that he needed work and work meant going west. He'd spent a few of the longest months of his life working on the construction of Hoover Dam. It was brutal, grueling—115-degree heat and backbreaking work. Men drowned, were crushed or just worked themselves to death. Jack knew there had to be something better. He left the camp called Ragtown and risked his future further west. He was damn lucky it paid off. He looked across the street and saw the studio gate where he'd stood, fresh off the train, hoping for a break. Felt like a lifetime ago.

Jack started to cross the street when he heard an odd sound coming from the alley between two buildings behind him. He stopped to listen—hushed voices and then a woman's cry of surprise. Jack felt the rush of adrenaline. Cries coming from alleys never meant anything good.

He ran back down the street. As he rounded into the mouth of the alley he saw a well-dressed woman being attacked. A man in a torn, shabby suit had her around the waist, squeezing her hard. Jack felt a flash of anger as he dashed down the alley. He ripped the man's arms off her waist and flung him aside. For his size, the big man went down easily. The man looked up at him with gaunt eyes, wide with surprise. Jack grabbed him by the frayed lapels of his dirty coat and hauled him to his feet.

"What the hell do you think you're doing?" Jack growled, his fist cocked and ready to send this chump into tomorrow afternoon. The other man raised his hands in surrender and Jack shoved him away in disgust. He fixed him with a glare that told the man he'd better not move a muscle and turned to make sure the woman was all right. What he saw was the last thing he expected and it hit him like a punch in the gut.

"Betty?"

WHEN ELIZABETH HAD FIRST arrived in California, she'd taken the Universal Studios tour. Riding a tram through a studio-cum-amusement park wasn't quite the same as rolling up in a limo to the main gate of Mammoth Studios with Alan Grant.

He was baffled at their interest in Sam Roth. "He's the least interesting man on the lot." But, Alan was pleased to acquiesce regardless and introduce them to the mogul after he'd given them a tour of the studio. He had to go to the studio to view the rushes from his latest picture and, it was clear to both Simon and Elizabeth, Alan didn't want to be alone.

On the way there, they'd planted the seed that Simon was between jobs and if Alan knew of anything at the studio that might tide them over for a bit, they'd be most beholden. Whether it was a job in the secretarial pool or blocking hats, it didn't really matter as long as it got them studio passes. That way, they could have access to the lot without having to rely on Grant. Between Ruby, Sam Roth and Alan, Mammoth Studios seemed like it might a good place to start looking for the source of the trouble.

The guard smiled broadly and let them through the main entrance. The enormous iron gates with the outline of rearing wooly mammoths on either side slowly closed behind them.

Elizabeth loved the movies and being in a real live studio, in the heart of the Golden Age of movies was almost too much. She barely resisted rolling down the window and sticking her head out as they drove down the main road between towering sound stages.

Eventually, Peter pulled the car over and Alan helped her out of the back seat. A group of men dressed as American Indians walked toward them. One of them pulled a box of cigarettes from his pocket and offered one to the chief. They greeted Alan with waves of their hands and thick Brooklyn accents as they passed.

Elizabeth giggled.

"Totally inaccurate," Simon said. "Apache headdress and Chumash markings. Ridiculous."

"And awesome," Elizabeth said. "This isn't a museum; this is the movies."

Peter brought a small basket of carnations around to Alan, who chose one and slipped it into his lapel buttonhole. "Shall we?" He checked his watch. "I have to be at the bridge at 3 p.m. That leaves us an hour or so for a cook's tour."

"Wonderful!"

Alan grinned, extended his hand and gestured for her to walk with him.

The studio was a city within a city. It covered multiple city blocks and the back lot spread out over acre upon acre. It was complete with it's own power plant and fire department. There were laundry facilities, multiple commissaries, housing, offices and even a school.

"It's a bit like a mad kingdom," Alan said. "A court where you can curry favor or lose it just as easily. There are jesters to entertain you and fools to tell you truths you'd rather not hear. Intrigue and secrets. Waste and want. Usurpers and honest men. It's a place where incompetence and genius are equally rewarded. Where the more lies you tell, the truer they become. It's false and vain and magic. This, my darling, is the movies. And I love it more than my very soul."

There was something about the way he said it that almost made her believe him. Maybe it was true in a way. She lost that train of thought when Alan called out to someone who bounded toward them and Elizabeth's mouth went dry.

Alan shook hands with the man and turned to introduce her. "Elizabeth Cross, I'd like you to meet, Cary Grant. No relation. He's a young star on his way up. Going to go damn far if I'm any judge."

After the words Cary Grant, the rest of what Alan said barely registered. She was drooling. She was pretty sure she was drooling. Oh my god, she wanted to crawl inside that cleft in his chin and never come out and he was talking to her.

"Hello," he said with that Cary Grant voice of his, although it was a bit boyish. He shook her hand brightly and grinned at Simon who grunted in response.

"Don't tell me Roth pried you out of Paramount already?" Alan asked.

Grant flashed a smile and laughed. Elizabeth's knees wobbled a little. She was probably still drooling but resisted the urge to feel her chin. All she could do was stare.

"Not yet," he said. "Although, I think I'd rather be here than there."

"Be careful what you wish for," Alan said. "Good seeing you."

Cary nodded and gave Elizabeth another smile. "Nice meeting you."

And with that, he was gone and her hand was still tingling. Alan laughed and waved a hand in front of her face. She finally snapped out of it.

"Oh, yes," Alan said. "He's going to do all right." He took Elizabeth's arm. "Do you need smelling salts?"

Elizabeth giggled nervously. "No. I'm fine. It was just…" She looked after him and then back to Simon who was impatiently waiting for her explanation. She offered him a weak smile, which he did not return. She spun around and pointed at a building. "So that's the laundry…"

Alan wrapped her arm through his and led her to a nondescript door that said: Publicity Dept. "Very important, people. They paint the posters and create all of the advertising for a picture. There was an unfortunate mishap at a Christmas party that resulted in, well, a less than flattering painting of me adorning Sunset Blvd. You must continuously grease the wheels, as it were."

He let go of her arm and she and Simon stood in the doorway of a large office/workspace where several artists were busily creating, painting and sketching images for upcoming Mammoth releases. Alan greeted the two men with slaps on the back and then dipped in front of an older woman. She didn't smile at first, but he said something that broke through her barrier. It was fascinating to see him work his magic.

Alan took the carnation from his lapel, pretended to smell it and dramatically handed it to her with a courtly bow. The woman, taciturn just minutes ago, blushed and giggled like a schoolgirl. With a sweep of his hand Alan bid her adieu and shuttled them all out of the office. "One down," he said.

Peter approached them and held out the basket of carnations. Alan took another and slipped it into his buttonhole. "Purchasing next, I think."

Alan repeated the same scene to several women in different departments. From the steno pool like set-up of purchasing to the lone woman manning the stacks and stacks of scripts in the script department, he greeted them, made them smile and "spontaneously" gave them the flower from his jacket. Each of them felt special and positively glowed when he left.

Between giftings, he dutifully explained what each department did.

"Aren't you afraid they'll compare notes? The women?" Elizabeth asked. "Realize they aren't the only one?"

"Ah, but that's the beauty of it," Alan said as he escorted them into yet another building complex. "Each and every flower is sincerely given. In that moment, they *are* the only woman."

Simon rolled his eyes and Elizabeth took his hand as they followed after Grant.

The final flower was delivered to a tall, buck-toothed woman in the wardrobe department, which was amazing. Racks upon racks of every imaginable type of clothing filled an enormous warehouse. Clothes were hung three levels high and Elizabeth could hear the hum of sewing machines in the adjacent room. People hurried down the aisles and used long hooks to bring down clothes from the upper levels. A woman with an armful of 18th century French silk coats hurried past and a man pushed a cart with Roman Centurion helmets on it.

They emerged into the sunlight again and Alan led them back between towering sound stages. Extras and bit players in every imaginable costume hurried past. The trio rounded a corner and was nearly swallowed whole by a dozen dancing girls. They flocked to Alan like birds to a nest, their feathered headdresses and bustles and boobs bouncing as they took turns saying hello and cooing over him. Elizabeth jostled around inside the crowd, a cloud of feathers obscuring her vision.

And like a flock of birds, they swept on past, leaving the three of them in their wake. Alan took out a handkerchief and grinned after them. His face was covered with lipstick. He happily rubbed it off. "Never let a woman see you with someone else's lipstick on your face."

He turned to Simon. "You have a bit..." he said with a broad grin.

Simon's cheeks were nearly as covered with bright red kisses as Alan's had been.

Elizabeth cleared her throat and Simon reached up and touched his cheek, surprised when his fingers came away covered with lip rouge. "It happened so fast, I didn't even realize..."

"Uh-huh."

Alan laughed loudly. "And now to the lion's den."

CHAPTER NINE

IT HAD BEEN YEARS since he'd seen her, but he'd never forgotten her. Could never forget her. Betty. She'd broken his heart in 1938 and he was never a whole man again. And yet here she was.

His mouth went dry and his heart beat out a conga against his ribs. Years ago, when he'd gone to war, he'd given up any hope of seeing her again. But he'd never forgotten her, not an inch of her. Not her smile or her hair or her kindness.

"You idiot!" Betty glared at him before maneuvering around him and going to check on the man Jack had almost clocked. She touched the man's arm and looked up into his unshaven face. "Are you all right?"

The man gave Jack an uneasy glance before nodding and pushing himself up and off the wall and upright.

Jack could hardly believe his eyes. It really was Betty. She was younger than he remembered, but, of course, she would be. This was four or five years before they'd even met. God, she was beautiful. Light brown hair that looked like gold when the sun hit it. Brown eyes that flashed when she got angry and that adorable little dimple in her chin.

For a moment, Jack wondered if she'd remember him. Would it be fondly or just a fading memory. That's when he realized the truth of it. Of course, she wouldn't recognize him; for her, they hadn't even met yet. He tried to make sense of the paradox. He was his older self, meeting her before his younger self had even had the chance. Damn, younger Jack had managed to screw it up. Not that she gave him much of a chance, but what he wouldn't give to have another. She was kind and wonderful and…yelling at him.

"Listen, you big palooka, I don't know what you think you were doing—"

"I'm sorry," Jack said, trying to concentrate on the now. She was standing between him and the man, her brown eyes flashing as she jabbed at his chest.

"Well," she said, brought up a little short by his quick apology. "You should be."

"I really am sorry," Jack said. "I thought he was attacking you."

"Didn't get hugged much as a child, did you?" she said.

It was all he could do not to laugh. That was pure Betty—sharp, funny, incisive, beautiful.

"He was thanking me," she continued as though she were speaking to a backwards child. "I brought him and his family some things from the studio to tide them over."

That's when Jack noticed the rest of the family and he felt a hot flush of guilt. The man's wife looked terrified, ready to bolt, but standing her ground, arms around her two small children who were torn between excitement and horror. Their clothes were torn and old, and dirty. The woman's dress was several sizes too large for her and hung off her thin body like it was no more than a hanger in a closet. Next to them, on the discarded crates in the alley was a small box of clothing, a new pair of Mary Janes sitting on top.

Jack quickly took off his hat and pressed it against his chest. He shook his head in apology and addressed the wife. "I'm sorry, ma'am. I didn't mean to frighten you. Any of you," he added to the kids. The girl curled into her mother's leg and the boy stuck his tongue out at him. Jack gave a quick laugh. "Good for you, kid."

Jack turned back and Betty sized him up. "Maybe there's hope for you yet."

Jack's heart stuttered. He knew she hadn't meant it the way he wanted to hear it, but a chance was a chance and he wasn't going to miss this one. "I sure hope so," he said softly. Then, he stepped forward and held out his hand to the man. "I am *very* sorry."

The man looked at Jack's hand. The world had kicked him in the seat of the pants so often he'd learned not to trust anyone or anything. But even after all the abuse the Depression had doled out, he still had the pride innate in every man. He straightened up to his full height and shook Jack's hand. "S'okay."

"I'd like to make it up to you," Jack said. "To all of you." He struggled with what to do.

The man walked over to his family and stood behind his wife. His dirty hand came to rest on her shoulder and Jack saw an inspiring strength in their unity. "You don't have to do nothin', Mister. We're all right."

The lie and the courage it took to tell went straight to Jack's heart. "Let me at least buy you lunch. There's a great hot dog place just down the street. I'm starving and I bet," he said looking at the little boy, "you like your dogs with mustard and relish. Am I right? I'm a mustard and relish man myself."

The little boy licked his lips and looked anxiously up at his parents—a silent plea in his shadowed eyes. The couple was clearly uncomfortable at the offer, but in dire need of the help.

"Just lunch," Jack said. "Everybody's gotta eat, right? And uhm," he leaned in conspiratorially, "it might help me make up some points with the pretty lady."

"Who is standing right here and can hear everything you're saying."

Jack grinned. "See? Tough nut to crack. You sure would be helpin' me out."

Betty rolled her eyes, but despite it all, she smiled. The man looked down at his wife and children and finally over to Betty before nodding. "We'd be most obliged, mister."

Their scraggly little parade headed out of the alley and down the block toward the hot dog vendor on the corner. Jack tried not to keep looking over at Betty, but he couldn't stop himself. She was there, alive and at his side. A living, breathing second chance at happiness.

When he'd first met her in 1938, he'd seen her at a party and fallen in love with her from across the room. When his friend had introduced them, for the first time in his life, he didn't know what to say to a woman. She was smart and funny and kind and a little wounded. And he'd never seen anyone more beautiful. He'd met movie stars and models and even dated more than his share, but something about Betty went straight to and through his heart. He pursued her relentlessly in the months that followed, finally wearing her down, against her better judgment, she'd said. Their affair was wonderful until she pushed him away.

After that, he'd joined the Navy and heard that she'd left Los Angeles. Last he'd heard she was married and living in San Francisco. But she wasn't there now. She was here. And he was here. And he had another chance and he wasn't going to waste it.

He could hear Cross' voice in the back of his mind warning him about affecting the timeline, but Jack shut him out. If Cross has been in his shoes and this was Elizabeth.... Some things were worth the risks. He glanced over at Betty, who must have felt him staring and turned to look up at him. Her expression was wary, but curious. That pain that had kept her from him wasn't there. He smiled down at her and when she smiled back cautiously, he was lost. Whatever it took, whatever the risks, he wouldn't lose her this time.

The little boy ran ahead and his mother called out to him. "David!"

David turned around and hunched his shoulders and tilted his head back and opened his mouth in the universal body language of "come on, you are sooo slow." Betty and Jack exchanged smothered grins.

Jack ordered food for the family first. Once they had their dogs, he ordered one for himself and then one for Betty. "Mustard on half and ketchup on the other." As soon as he'd done it he knew he'd made a mistake. It was a reflex.

She looked at him curiously. "How'd you know I like mine like that?"

He accepted the dog from the vendor and handed it to her. "Lucky guess. You need more relish, David?"

The little boy, whose cheeks were so full they looked about to pop, shook his head and crammed another bite into his mouth. The little girl gave her mother her bun and nibbled her dog like a mouse working a piece of cheese.

"Kids," Jack said with a grin toward a still staring Betty. He took a bite of his own dog and smiled back innocently.

Once he was sure they'd all had their fill, he ordered four more. "For later," he said and stuffed them into his jacket pocket before slipping the coat off. He'd seen the state of the man's coat, holes in the pockets, threadbare sleeves.

He held it out to the father who looked at it hesitantly. Clearly, he was a proud man torn between honor and need.

"Here," Jack continued. "When things turnaround for you, you can help somebody else who needs it. Take it."

The man's jaw worked to hide his emotion. He finally nodded sharply and took the coat.

"Thank you," his wife said, lifting their daughter onto her hip. The little girl had only eaten half of her hotdog and gave the rest to her brother. She was a pale little thing and the way she rested her head against her mother's shoulder sent a pang of worry through Jack's system.

He didn't have much money with him, but he started to dig into his pocket. Betty's gentle hand on his arm stilled him. She smiled sadly and shook her head. Her eyes said she understood, but any more "generosity" would be unwelcome. Jack nodded and wished the family well as they left. The little boy ran alongside his father, trying to peek into his bulging pockets.

"That was very kind of you," Betty said once they were out of earshot. Then she turned and looked up at him with narrowed eyes. "What's your angle?"

Jack remembered that she was a world-class skeptic, but this Betty still had some faith in her fellow man.

"They needed help. I could give it," he added with a shrug.

Betty's eyes narrowed even more as she sized him up. She was good at that. When he'd met her, she was working for a big shot producer at one of the studios. The indispensable Girl Friday who could see right through the baloney.

"I think you really mean that," she said, sounding both impressed and a little incredulous.

"What you see is what you get." Although that was a big fat lie considering the circumstances, it was true in his heart.

Betty's brown eyes searched his face. "That'd be a first. Mister...?"

"J-John," he said quickly realizing he couldn't give her his real name and offered her the first one he could think of. "John West," he said holding out his hand.

She took it, but he could tell she was far from won over. "Betty Chase."

Jack couldn't have kept the grin off his face if he tried. "Nice to meet you, Betty Chase."

SIMON BARELY HAD TIME to wipe the lipstick from his cheek before Grant led them off to God knew where. That seemed to be a developing theme. As usual, Elizabeth was happy just to be along for the ride. Simon, however, took a more circumspect view of things and watched Grant's interactions with care. Whatever the threat to him, it could come from inside the studio. And while Sam Roth and his brother Benny were leading candidates for the role, it would be foolish to ignore the myriad women Grant dallied with. A woman with a broken heart was a dangerous thing and it appeared Grant broke hearts with some regularity.

Finally, Grant led them to what appeared to be the main building. It was five or six stories high and was large enough to cover a city block all by itself. A plush lawn stretched out in front of it. On one part of the grounds, a small unit of police officers stood in formation as what looked like Shirley Temple and a small film crew gave them an inspection.

The unbridled energy of the rest of the studio fell into silence inside the building. This was obviously the main office complex and it wasn't all fun and games in here; it was business. This was the front line in the constant battle between art and commerce and it was impressive. Oversized portraits of stars lined the walls, plush carpets lined the floors and money lined everything else. This was a show of wealth and power. It was there to inspire and intimidate.

As was typical, Grant was greeted with toothy smiles and over-excited hellos as they made their way up to the top floor. The art deco elevator dinged their arrival and they stepped out into the foyer.

An attractive, middle-aged woman who sat behind a modern-looking white semi-circular desk rose to meet them. "Mr. Roth will be right with you, Mr. Grant. Coffee, tea?"

"No, thank you, Ruth," Grant said and gestured for Elizabeth to sit down while they waited.

The upper lobby was surprisingly sparsely furnished. Where the lower lobby had been all show, this was nearly all business—few frills and the hush of hard work were even more intimidating than the spectacle downstairs.

The quiet efficiency was shattered by a loud voice from behind the doors to Roth's office.

"Damn it, Sam!" The door opened and Benny Roth stood in the doorway. "You're my goddamn brother."

Sam Roth appeared next to him, his face ruddy with anger and was about to say something when he noticed he had an audience. He rolled his shoulders to try to dispel some of his seething anger and fixed his little brother with eyes that brooked no nonsense. "Later."

Benny Roth opened his mouth to protest, but a fierce glare from his brother shut it with a snap. He stormed out of the office nearly running into Grant in his rush. He growled something at Grant and shoved him bodily out of the way. Elizabeth was immediately out of her chair and ready to intervene, but Simon put a hand to her arm.

Grant played it off as though it were nothing as Roth stabbed the down elevator button. Benny Roth turned back to glare at his brother, but caught sight of Simon and Elizabeth. His expression was angry and filled with wanting something he couldn't have. There was a wildness in his eyes, a panic Simon recognized. He'd seen it in Ruby's eyes that night at the Biltmore. There was something else in Roth's eyes though. Simon couldn't put a name to it, but it was trouble. Whatever was taking Roth down, he wasn't going to go down easily. If he had to take someone with him, he would without blinking an eye.

Benny Roth grunted as the elevator arrived and he stepped inside. "This isn't over yet," he said. "I'll find one." It didn't seem aimed at his brother so much as the entire room, or maybe just himself.

Sam Roth watched the elevator doors close and huffed out a breath. It took him a moment to recover, and then the calm business like façade was securely back in place. "Grant?" he said impatiently. "We got rushes in ten. What are you doing here?"

"So lovely to you see you, Samuel," Grant said. "I wanted to introduce you to a few friends."

"You know the rules, Grant. Friendship," he said pointing at the threshold to his office, "stops here."

"Yes, of course," Grant said, clapping an unwanted hand on Roth's shoulder and escorting him into his own office. "They're actually here in search of work. Business, you see."

Grant waved behind his back, urging them to follow him.

He walked Roth into the middle of his large but utilitarian office. The only real decoration was a pair of massive curved tusks mounted to the floor behind Roth's desk and arching over his leather chair.

"They're…writers," Grant said with a quick flashing grin. "Gifted scenarists."

Roth turned to look at them. "Yeah?"

When they'd asked Grant to try to get them work at the studio this was hardly what Simon had expected.

"Talented playwrights from…" Grant started.

"London." "Texas."

Roth's brow creased and he pursed his lips.

Immediately they both answered again, but this time in reverse. "Texas." "London."

Grant glared at them and then clapped Roth on the shoulder again. "That's a comedic bit they're working on."

"They need to keep working," Roth said.

"Yes," Grant said with a sharp look. "But they are terribly talented."

Roth was unimpressed.

"And willing to work for peanuts."

"Circus peanuts even," Elizabeth added.

Roth's implacable expression was unmoved. He looked at Grant again, seeming to calculate exactly what it would cost him and the net return in having a happy star. The numbers must have fallen in their favor because he nodded. "Have them report to Miller. And fix that bit. S'not funny."

"Right!" Grant said.

They were just about to turn to leave when a voice from a darkened corner of the office stopped them. "Aren't you going to introduce me?"

The man's face was obscured by cigarette smoke caught in the dim light of a reading lamp. Instead of waving it away, he stood, pushing through it and emerging into the light. The effect was chilling and so was the man. Tall, slender and neatly dressed, he had a handsome enough face, sharp symmetrical features and keen dark eyes. But there was something unnerving about him, about the way he moved, the way his eyes took in the room that sent a shiver up Simon's spine. And yet, the man was familiar. It took Simon a moment to place him. Then he realized this was the man sitting at Grant's table at Musso & Frank.

Sam Roth frowned and picked up a cigar stub from the ashtray on his desk. "Thorn, these are…" he struggled disinterested and preoccupied. He waved a hand at Grant.

Grant's expression was the same as it always was, a casual smile, but there was none of the usual joy behind it. It was forced, tight.

"Perhaps another time," Grant said, moving to hurry Elizabeth from the room.

"I think this is a most opportune time," the man said moving between them and the door. He held out his hand. "Edgar Thorn. And you are?"

"Elizabeth Cross." She shook his hand briefly, but when she tried to let go, he pulled her a little closer. Simon instinctively started toward them, but a warning hand from Grant kept him from intervening.

"You are," Thorn said, seeming to look for the word in her eyes, "lovely. So…pure."

Thorn regarded Simon for a brief moment, a flash of a smile touching his eyes as their gazes met. Thorn might have been speaking to Elizabeth but it was really Simon he was talking to. It was a strange feeling, but Simon was sure of that. Just as he was sure this man was dangerous. He couldn't put his finger on what it was, but every instinct in his body was warning him that something was wrong. Something was very wrong.

Thorn turned his gaze back to Elizabeth and released her hand. He smiled affably. "Newlyweds?"

"How did you know?" she asked, sounding impressed.

Thorn lifted a long index finger and pointed it at Simon. "He doesn't like another man touching his wife. Only a newly married man cares that much about something so trivial. In a few years, he won't even notice," he added. "Isn't that right, Sam?"

Sam Roth had been watching from behind his desk. To Thorn's question, he merely grunted in reply, turning the cigar in his mouth.

"You should go," Grant said, taking Elizabeth by the hand and leading her toward Simon and the door.

Thorn smiled genially. "Of course. So much work to do." His eyes caught Simon's. "So good to see you again. I'm sure we'll see each other again soon."

Grant ushered them to the door. "You two go ahead. I'll catch you up downstairs."

Simon didn't need to be told twice and put his hand on Elizabeth's back to urge her along. The elevator door was open and waiting for them in the foyer. Once the doors had closed behind them, Simon turned to Elizabeth. "Didn't you feel it?"

"Feel what?"

Simon frowned. "Thorn. There's something about that man. I don't like it."

"I thought he was kind of creepy that night at Musso & Frank, but it must have just been the excitement of if all. Today, he seemed kind of interesting."

Simon stared at her in disbelief. Of the two of them, Elizabeth was supposed to be the intuitive one. How could she possibly have missed the menace that man exuded? "Interesting?" he asked, incredulous.

Elizabeth shrugged. She seemed completely unfazed and, worse yet, completely unaware of what Simon had perceived.

He turned her so that he could look into her eyes. She didn't look drugged. "Are you feeling all right?"

She shrugged again. "I'm a little hungry."

"Promise me," Simon said and waited until he had her full and undivided attention, "promise me that you won't be alone with that man. No dinners."

"Jealous?" she said playfully, but quickly saw this was no joke. "I promise."

Simon sighed and the elevator reached the ground floor. As they walked outside, his own feelings on the matter felt a little ridiculous. Maybe it had all been in his head? He just wasn't sure. Now, his reaction to the man felt overly dramatic, but there was a niggling voice in the back of his mind that wouldn't stay quiet.

Elizabeth slipped her arm into his. "Anyway, he didn't seem that bad to me."

"You would see the good in the devil himself," he said.

"Nobody's all bad."

Simon was not so sure.

Chapter Ten

THE FEW MINUTES THEY spent waiting outside for Alan turned into ten and Elizabeth busied herself by trying to figure out what had gotten into Simon. *Don't be alone with him. No dinners.* Where the Heckle and Jekyll had that come from? It wasn't like she was in the habit of having dinner with strange men. She'd had one measly dinner with a gangster vampire and Simon just wouldn't let it go.

Thorn was a smooth talker and attractive enough, if the silky smooth snaky sort was your type. But really, Simon's reaction to him was odd. She was just about to ask him about it when Alan came out of the building and hurried down the stairs to meet them.

"I'm afraid, I've got to dash to rushes. I'll see you in the commissary in an hour or so. The writer's building is that dilapidated one over there. See a man named Miller and he'll get you studio passes and then you can do what writers do," Grant added as he started to walk away.

"Write?" Elizabeth asked. "I don't know how to write."

"Have you read the script for latest film? Hasn't stopped them. Have fun!" he waved over his shoulder and was gone.

They didn't need the job, but having a studio pass that would allow them access to the lot could be valuable. They agreed to put in an appearance and pray they weren't given an assignment.

The writers' building was just across the lawn, but unlike the main building with Roth's offices, it had no pretense. It barely had paint. A group of men played dice in the hallway and Simon had to help Elizabeth step around them. It felt more like a frat house than an office building.

"Miller?" Simon asked.

One of the men on the floor jabbed a thumb toward the ceiling. "Third floor."

Elizabeth looked for the elevator, but didn't find one. There was, however, a broad open staircase. As she looked up, two men and a tiny woman with short dark hair were deep in conversation as they walked down the last flight.

Elizabeth's elbow jabbed Simon in the stomach so hard he let out a yelp. "What on earth—"

"Dorothy Parker," she whispered, pointing at the woman's back.

Simon turned to try to catch a glimpse of her, but a boy with a stack of papers leapt down the stairs and nearly collided with him. "Sorry, mister," the boy said and ran down the hall.

Elizabeth mouthed a "wow" and squelched a delighted giggle. Simon gestured for her to start up the stairs.

Miller's office was a jungle of paper. Piles of scripts teetered on the edge of toppling over. An attractive, busty woman in a tight skirt and even tighter sweater sat perched on the desk filing her nails. Her platinum blonde hair was nearly blinding. She popped her gum and stared at them blankly. Two cigarettes burned in the ashtray next to her.

Standing behind the desk was a tall man, or one who would have been if he ever straightened, but he seemed permanently bent. His graying hair was in disarray, his suit as rumpled as his face.

"Are you Miller? Simon asked.

The man squinted.

"Roth sent us," Elizabeth supplied. "We're writers."

Miller didn't look so sure. "Scenarists or dialogue?" he asked using his cigarette like an index finger, punctuating each question with a stab of it. "Are you funny? Can you tell me a joke? Tell me a joke."

Elizabeth looked anxiously at Simon. Although she would have paid good money to see Simon tell a joke, she cleared her throat, spread her feet to shoulder width and started. "A guy walks into a bar with a duck on his head—"

Miller waved it away. "You'll do."

He narrowed his eyes at Simon. "You a team?"

"Yes," Elizabeth said excitedly. She knew they weren't actually going to write anything, but it was still thrilling.

"Does it talk or is it just through you?"

"I'm quite capable of speaking for myself," Simon said.

"English," Miller said with a sour face. "That's all I need. All right, I got plenty of crap that needs punching up. What about that jungle thing with Grant, that uhm—"

"*Through the Dark Continent*?" Elizabeth answered. That was exciting and a little troubling. *Through the Dark Continent* was the last movie Grant ever made. After it, he just dropped off the map. The movie was unfinished and never released.

Miller slammed his hand down on the desk and frowned in distaste. "That's the one. Do something with it. Fix it."

Elizabeth was stunned. "Really?"

"We were told we'd need studio passes. Where do we procure those?" Simon asked, bringing her back on point.

"Procure them?" Miller said and then looked up to his ceiling. "Why'd it have to be an Englishman?" He glared at Elizabeth. "You're American, right?"

"Texan."

"Close enough. Now get out."

He waved them away. The woman on the desk smiled amiably at them, handed them a few wrinkled forms and blew a bubble with her gum. "Downstairs. 201," she said with another loud pop of her gum.

After wandering through the halls, they found room 201 and the main writers' room. It wasn't that hard actually, thanks to the sound of a dozen or so Underwood typewriters banging away and the rumble of loud voices. Half a dozen desks held a dozen men and a few women. Some worked away hunched over their typewriters, others were talking animatedly and one was throwing a rubber ball against the wall. A cloud of smoke hovered above them almost obscuring the pincushion ceiling where dozens of pencils dangled down.

Simon introduced himself and Elizabeth to the haggard-looking man who seemed to be in charge, if anyone could have said to have been. He took the papers Simon had, crumpled them into balls and threw them into an enormous pile of balled up paper in the corner. He gave Simon fresh paperwork to fill out and Elizabeth used the opportunity to see what she could find out about Ruby or Roth.

Most people were in heated arguments or busy working. One man was asleep on his desk, curled up like a small child between his pencil sharpener and typewriter.

"I wouldn't get too close," a man said from behind her. He looked like a fox. His nose was long and sharp, his eyes small and dark; he even had tawny hair. "It's better upwind."

He escorted Elizabeth away from the sleeping man toward his desk. Another writer, with owlish glasses and a round face looked up from his work, which Elizabeth realized was blacking out teeth on movie star headshots. "Ohh, a girl," he said with a grin, forgetting his drawings. "Show me your legs."

"Charlie," said Mr. Fox.

"What? I miss my wife. She's been gone to Florida for two weeks. Just a little leg? An ankle?"

Elizabeth liked him; she liked them both, the owl and the fox. She put one leg out and inched up the hem to show off her calf. Wolf whistles came from men who weren't even looking. She could feel the heat of Simon's glare from across the room.

Charlie shook his head. "Nothing like my wife's."

Mr. Fox lifted his pant leg to reveal a pale hairy calf.

"Now *that* looks like my wife!"

Elizabeth laughed, much to the delight of both Charlie and Mr. Fox, who held out a chair for her.

"Thank you." As she sat down, she noticed today's issue of *Variety* on Charlie's desk.

"Pretty shocking about that girl, isn't it?" she said.

"Ruby?" Charlie picked up the paper and then tossed it aside. "Yeah." There was a decided lack of surprise in his voice.

"Or not so shocking?" she asked.

"It's a shame and all; she was pretty, even had a little talent, but there was just somethin' about that dame."

Mr. Fox picked up the paper. "You just don't like Benny Roth."

"He waters down his gin!" Charlie said indignantly and then shrugged it off. "I don't know. One day, she's a nobody; the next day the whole town can't fall over themselves fast enough to give her the world on a silver platter. Heard maybe she had something going with Roth on the side."

"Sam?" Mr. Fox said. "The only thing he likes to make love to is his money."

Simon joined them and Elizabeth introduced him to Charlie and Mr. Fox.

"They were just telling me about Sam Roth," Elizabeth said.

Simon sat down on the edge of the desk. "Were those actual wooly mammoth tusks in his office?"

"The real McCoy," Charlie said. "Story is he found them himself, when he was looking for oil."

"Oil?" Elizabeth asked.

"Studios don't come cheap ya know," Charlie said. "That's how Roth got his money. Another overnight sensation you might say."

"How so?" Simon prompted.

"Story is, he came here, what 30 years ago, young kid from the East coast looking for a pot of gold at the end of the rainbow. Found it at Wilshire Boulevard."

"The La Brea Tar Pits," Elizabeth said more to herself than the men. She'd visited them the last time she'd come to LA—huge pools of tar or asphalt bubbling up from enormous deposits of crude oil. That explained all of the oil derricks they'd seen downtown.

"Right," Charlie said. "Supposedly, he hooked up with Thorn and they somehow managed to beat Standard Oil and the rest of them out of one of the richest oil fields in California."

"And he found the mammoth tusks in a tar pit above the oil," Simon reasoned. "Hence the name Mammoth Studios."

Charlie touched his nose. "Give that man a cheroot. Thorn stayed a silent partner and Roth founded the studio. And here we are wasting his not-so-hard earned money."

"Gets ya right here," Mr. Fox said touching his heart. "And a little down here," he added touching his stomach and pretending to belch.

LIFE DIDN'T GIVE OUT second chances very often. Jack had been lucky enough to have more than his fair share. The fact that he was alive and kicking was testament to that. It was unnerving to think of the number of times he could have and should have died. If Simon and Elizabeth hadn't literally pulled his bacon out of the fire in 1942, his story would have ended, like so many others, at the point of the German bomb. And now, life had given him yet another go. He'd be damned if he was going to let it pass him by.

Jack paid the taxi driver and walked the last block west toward the setting sun. He'd managed to convince Betty to meet him for dinner. It had taken some doing. Even this younger, hopeful version of Betty was a bit of a cynic—a funny, wonderful, heart beneath the armor of a cynic. Hollywood taught you that people who wore their hearts on their sleeves didn't survive. By the time Jack had met Betty in 1938 and fallen head over heels for her, she'd learned that the hard way. But this Betty didn't look at him and see the shadow of the man who'd hurt her. For the first time, she could look at him and just see him.

Of course, he thought, the real him was using a fake name and couldn't tell her who he really was or why he was really here. Starting off with a fistful of lies was far from ideal, but he'd learned in the spy game that circumstances were never ideal, and you did the best with what you had. He'd also learned to focus on today and not tomorrow. Tomorrow was never guaranteed. And, for Jack, today meant a second chance with the woman who stole his heart and that was all that mattered.

He saw her leaning against the fence that lined the bluffs above the Roosevelt Highway and the Pacific Ocean below. God, she was beautiful. The light from the setting sun cast a golden hue across everything it touched. It seemed to linger just a little bit longer on her, touching her hair, caressing her cheek.

She turned and gave him a small wave. His heart pounded in his chest. He felt like a teenage boy on his first date. It was horrifying. And it was wonderful.

"I hope you haven't been waiting long," he said.

She smiled and shook her head. "No," she said turning back to watch the sunset. "I forget how beautiful the ocean is. I'm still not used to seeing it."

He moved next to her and leaned forward, resting his elbows on top of the fence. "Not a native then?" he asked, already knowing the answer.

She laughed. "Is anyone? Nope, I'm from Fort Wayne, Indiana."

"You're a long way from home."

Betty looked out at the sun dipping beneath the far horizon. "Yeah. A long way."

Jack searched her face for a clue to the sadness he heard in her voice. "Homesick?"

She held out her hand, thumb and forefinger about an inch apart. "A little."

Jack shifted his weight onto his left elbow and turned toward her. "You know what does wonders for homesickness?"

She gave him a skeptical smile.

"Ice cream."

She laughed, but he continued, "It's a scientific fact. There's a great place just down on the pier."

"We haven't even had dinner yet."

He shrugged. "After dinner then? For medicinal purposes only, of course."

She smiled. "I am feeling pretty homesick. I might need a double."

"That can be arranged."

Dinner at Luigi's went past in a blur. Betty was a strange and wonderful mixture of things—smart and funny and ready to sock the world right in the kisser with one hand and pull it to her with the other. The years he'd spent dreaming about her, wondering where she was, if she was happy, if she had children now, fell back into the dark in their candle-lit corner booth.

His memory had painted gauzy pictures of the past. But no memory, not even ones that had kept him going during some of the darkest nights of the war, compared to this, to being with her again. It seemed impossible, but she was even lovelier than he'd remembered.

He knew it was foolish. He knew it couldn't be. And yet, he couldn't stop himself from dreaming, from hoping against hope there was a way to stay together. If she'd even have him, he realized. He loved her, had always loved her, but to Betty he was a stranger. Maybe she'd send him away and that would be that. All he knew was, he had to find out if she could, if she would love him. And if she did, he would find a way. There was always a way.

After dinner, they walked along a busy Ocean Park enjoying the warm spring evening. Even the wind coming in off the ocean was gentle and warm. They fell in with the crowd and headed down the long sloping entrance that led to the mouth of the Santa Monica Pier. In the distance the sound of a band organ playing something vaguely circus-like came ashore with the wind.

At the base of the long ramp, a large two-story red and yellow building stood where the pier met the end of the bluff. Tall Spanish Colonial spires jutted out over arched Byzantine windows in a strange menagerie of styles. As they walked closer to the open archways that spread across the first floor, the music grew louder and was joined with bright flashes of light.

Jack nodded toward the carousel asking if she wanted to ride. She smiled and shook her head. They contented themselves with watching others climb aboard the colorful hand-carved horses. Mothers held on to their children, men held on to their dates and some held on to their lunches as the enormous carousel started up again. After a few minutes, Jack put his hand on the small of Betty's back and led her out back into the night air and further down the pier.

He maneuvered them through the crowd to a small storefront. "Your medicine," he said, gesturing to the blackboard with today's special ice cream flavors.

They both opted for a single scoop cone of chocolate and then found an out-of-the-way bench and sat. As they worked on their cones in contented silence, they watched the crowd pass by.

"You've got a little..." Betty said pointing at Jack's face.

He wiped his chin with a paper napkin, but she shook her head. He tried again only to have her laugh and reach toward him. With the pad of her thumb, she gently rubbed a spot just under his lower lip. Her eyes focused on his mouth; her own lips slightly parted as she wiped away the errant drop of chocolate. It was completely innocent and yet it made the blood rush out of his brain. Once she'd finished, she sat back against the bench and he continued to stare at her like some escapee. He sat there slack-jawed, aching to kiss her and knowing he couldn't.

"Are you all right?" she asked, narrowing her eyes with concern.

"Dancing?" he said before his brain had started fully functioning again. "Me."

She cocked her head to the side and then spoke to him like he was a backwards child. She pointed at the bench. "Sitting. Dancing different."

He laughed. "Right. I mean, do you dance?" It was another cheat. He knew the answer. She loved to dance.

She hesitated.

He knew that look in her eyes; he'd seen it so many times. She was teetering on the edge of saying yes and just one more little nudge would do it. "If you're a little clumsy, that's okay. I don't mind if you step on my feet."

"Oh, you don't mind?" There was a tinge to her voice that meant she was winding up.

"Well, you do have pretty big feet for a girl." He pointed down at her perfectly normal feet.

"I do not!" She was about to lay into him when she realized he was joking. Her pique melted into an embarrassed smile.

He stood and held out his hand to help her up. She looked at it warily for a minute before accepting. They walked a little further down the pier to the La Monica Ballroom. It was enormous and spread out across the width of the double pier. It was another mishmash of styles that seemed to find a home in LA. The outside was Spanish-style stucco with a dozen twenty-foot minarets dotting the perimeter. Each minaret top, like something out of Ali Baba, was lit by hundreds of tiny fairy lights and made the whole building look like some insane magic palace that had floated across both oceans and time and plopped down right in the middle of the pier.

Betty, who had never been to La Monica's, stopped outside and stared at the building. "That makes no sense."

Jack put her arm through his. "Sense is overrated."

The interior was equally bizarre and wonderful. The cavernous 15,000 square foot ballroom had entrances from every side and was ringed by a large open promenade with a café and fountain. There was even an upper level mezzanine with plush upholstered chairs and divans.

Jack bought them both tickets, just a dime these days. Back when Jack had first come, it was a dime for each dance and men with ropes would herd off each set of dancers when the music was over to make way to for the next set of paying customers. But, the Depression didn't spare anyone and La Monica cut its rates and even started offering dance marathons as a way to make enough money to keep the doors open.

Luckily, for him, one ticket bought a whole night of dancing, and Jack led Betty out in the throng that covered the maple dance floor. For a cynic, she had an incredibly wide-eyed with wonder look about her. She gazed up at the ceiling and the three-dozen bell-shaped chandeliers that dangled over them held by gold ropes. The large paintings on the walls depicted an underwater garden and it gave the entire room a feeling of being in a bubble beneath the sea.

When he found an open spot, Jack took Betty's hand and placed it on his shoulder. He smoothly took a hold of her other hand and they effortlessly fell in with the mass of dancers. Rogers and Hart's "You Are Too Beautiful" had just started and they moved slowly in time to the melancholy song.

Jack held Betty's off-hand high and tried to keep their bodies a respectable distance apart, but it was damn hard. He kept his hand on her back light and fought the temptation to pull her to him.

She caught him staring and ducked her eyes self-consciously. "I don't usually do this," she said, bringing her face up toward his. He arched an eyebrow and she smiled. "Go out with men I don't know."

"I know," he said, hoping she could see the sincerity of his feelings for her.

She started to say something else, but frowned.

"It's like dancing," he said. He spun them around in a graceful turn, her body moving with his as though they'd done it a thousand times. "You just have to go where the music takes you."

She smiled, half puzzled and half in wonder. "And where's that?"

He couldn't resist then and pulled her just a little closer. He brought his off-hand toward his chest and pressed the back of her hand over his heart. "There's only one way to find out."

CHAPTER ELEVEN

SIMON AND ELIZABETH SPENT the morning at the studio, os-
tensibly getting up to speed on Grant's picture, *Through the
Dark Continent.* Simon shuddered at the memory. The script
was dreadful. He'd been completely sincere and a little surprised
no one had appreciated his suggestion that the original writers
might perhaps benefit from remedial history and English lessons. Perhaps it had been a mercy that the film would never
see the light of day. It started off well enough, he supposed.
Alan played Henry Morton Stanley, explorer and journal-
ist, on his dangerous journey through the jungles of Africa in
search of the missing missionary Dr. David Livingstone. It was
faithful enough to reality until the famous "Dr. Livingstone, I
presume?" whereupon everything had gone pear shaped. He
blamed *King Kong.*

Now, instead of Livingstone staying to help the natives,
he stayed because he'd found the Great Dark Ape! He and

Stanley set out to capture the monster. It was derivative; it was shameless; it was Hollywood.

It was just as well it ended up on a shelf somewhere. It was beyond saving, Simon thought. He'd started to wonder if Alan Grant might be too. He and Elizabeth spent the remainder of the day trying to learn more about the people who had been with Grant that first night at Musso & Frank.

As Mr. Fox and Mr. Owl, as Elizabeth called them, had told them, Ruby's ascent from nobody to star was virtually rocket-propelled. And, her ascent to stardom coincided with meeting Benny Roth. That seemed to be a new wrinkle. Nearly everyone they spoke to was scared of Benny. They were scared the way children were scared of a bully. They wanted to tell you things, but didn't dare. It was clear that he was in financial trouble and that his brother refused to bail him out. That corresponded with what Jack told them on the phone last night. Benny Roth's bootlegging empire was slipping away from him.

Benny's brother Sam was well respected by most of the studio employees they spoke to, although, the writers seemed to have a more jaded view of him. His longtime connection with Thorn was troubling.

They'd tried to get a few of the secretaries in the main building to talk about Thorn, but they all said the same thing. "Isn't he charming?" "Oh, I don't really know anything about Mr. Thorn, but isn't he pleasant?" Everything about Mr. Thorn was vague. Vague and pleasant. Vague yes, but pleasant was hardly the word Simon would use. He was still bothered by their brief encounter with the man although he couldn't quite articulate why.

After nearly a full day spent, they were still no closer to understanding the threat to Alan Grant. As midday turned into afternoon, they decided to go to Grant's house and see if he was ready to share his secret.

Just as they were walking up the long drive to his mansion, the front door opened. Peter stood there with a young girl, no more than fourteen or fifteen. She argued with him and he placed a soothing hand on her shoulder. Her body trembled and she shook her head emphatically.

"I'm sorry," Peter said. "I tried. He won't see you."

"Please?" the young girl begged. "I know if he'll just see me—"

"I'm sorry, miss," Peter said and angled her out the door.

The girl buried her face in a handkerchief and ran down the steps. Elizabeth started to say something to her, but the girl hurried down the driveway. Peter watched her go. His usually impassive expression was filled with sadness and frustration. He stepped aside to let them in. "I'm afraid he's in a mood."

"Who was that?" Simon asked looking after the girl as she disappeared beyond the gate.

For a moment, Peter looked like he wanted to tell them, but he thought better of it. He gave one last look down the driveway and closed the door behind them. "Mr. Grant," he said in clipped, cold tones, "is in the library."

He looked at them once more before bowing and heading down the hall away from the library. Whatever was going on, it had bothered Peter enough for him to break form. The thought of the girl's face made Simon tense. What had Grant done?

Elizabeth knocked on the library door tentatively. "Alan?" Silence. After a moment, she knocked again. "It's Elizabeth and Simon."

There was another pause, so long they thought he might have left the room, but eventually they heard a quiet, "Come in."

Grant stood on the far side of the room looking out of the window, his hands clasped behind his back. He did not turn around to greet them.

Most people considered the kitchen the heart of a house. Simon guessed that was probably true, but if it was, the library was its soul. Grant's desk was devoid of paperwork. The books that lined the walls seemed to have been chosen more for their appearance than what was inside them. They were beautiful old leather volumes filled with dry material, probably as brittle as the pages they were written on. The whole room had the feeling of being designed and never lived in. What did that say, Simon wondered, about the man standing in front of them? And what of the girl? What had he done to her?

Elizabeth looked up to Simon with a worried expression. Grant hadn't moved or acknowledged them at all.

"Are you all right?" she asked.

"No."

His voice was so soft Simon wasn't sure he'd heard him.

"Alan?" Elizabeth said, clearly worried.

He turned and forced a smile onto his face. "Yes, of course, I'm fine."

The pain on his face was evident. Was there guilt there too?

"The girl who just left here wasn't," Simon said.

Grant's perpetual façade slipped just the tiniest bit. "No, she wasn't." His gaze darted to the photograph on his desk. There was nothing else personal in the room. Grant took two long strides, turned the photo face down and sat on the edge of the desk, blocking it from view. "But, she will be."

"You sound rather sure of that," Simon said. "Who was she?"

"No one for you to worry about."

Simon did worry. How could he not? He knew Hollywood mores were nearly non-existent, but this was too much. "She's just a child."

"I don't see what—" Grant started and then Simon's insinuation finally reached the gin-soaked recesses of his brain. "You don't think…"

"Simon," Elizabeth said, shocked.

"I assure you, it is not what you think," Grant said. "I would give my life to protect her," he added sadly. "If I had one to give."

Simon studied him carefully. For the first time, he believed Grant was telling him the truth, the whole truth, no theatrics, no embellishments, just a glimpse at his bare soul. What Simon hadn't expected was to recognize the pain in it. He himself had lived most of his life with it as a companion, keeping the rest of the world at bay.

"She is better off without me. Let's just leave it at that, shall we?" Grant said.

Elizabeth moved instinctively to comfort Grant, but he was still too raw. Simon knew that feeling as well.

Simon noticed some paperwork on the desk and a large, leather-bound book, *Black's Law Dictionary*. Simon arched an eyebrow.

Grant followed his gaze and smiled ruefully. "My will. For all the good it will do," he said softly as he slipped the book back onto the bookshelf.

"I could use a drink. Anyone else?" Grant added quickly, trying to avoid Elizabeth's kindness. He looked around for a drink cart or bottle of something. He opened desk drawers and closed them with a touch of anger. "Damn it."

"Don't use this room much?" Elizabeth asked, trying to give Grant room and time to recover.

She'd meant it lightly, but Grant stopped his search and regarded her sadly. "No. It's all the books." He waved at the bookshelves and she scanned the shelves. "They make you think. I'm better when I don't think too much. Introspection is a bit like castor oil. It might be good for you, but it's so difficult to swallow."

He opened and closed another series of cabinets. "Ah-ha!" he said in victory as he pulled a bottle and a few glasses from the recesses of a credenza. He poured himself a stiff drink.

"That won't help," Simon said from experience.

Elizabeth slowly approached Grant. "But we can. We know you're in trouble. Let us help you."

Alan lifted his glass and then set it down with a sigh. "Oh, my dear. If only you could. I'm just selfish enough to let you." He picked up his glass. "But, lucky for you, there's nothing to be done."

He downed two fingers of scotch in one gulp. "You can't save a man who's already dead."

JACK LEANED AGAINST THE wall and watched her. He'd spent years trying to remember every nuance of her—the way she tilted her head and wrinkled her forehead when she was self-conscious, the way she bit her lower lip in concentration, the way her body had felt against his as they'd danced.

Workers in the costume department hurried past with racks of clothes, the metal wheels squeaking in protest. Betty finally looked up, sensing someone was watching her, and he pushed off from the pillar he'd been leaning against and lifted the bouquet of flowers in his hand as a greeting. When she smiled, his heart stuttered.

"Hello," she said, the hint of a blush touching her cheeks.

He handed her the flowers. "Picked them myself."

She frowned in disbelief until she saw the clump of dirt hanging off one of the stems. She fought down a smile. "Don't these grow around the commissary?"

He offered her his broadest grin. "Some still do."

She gave up the fight and let her laugh bubble out. "You're impossible."

No, he thought. Nothing was impossible.

ALAN HAD CLOSED OFF quickly after the incident with the girl at his house. Elizabeth had tried to get him to talk to them, but he'd all but sent them away. She'd seen the look in his eye though. Despite his words, he wasn't ready to give up. There was still hope. She had to believe there was always hope.

She planned on working on him again tonight. They'd all been invited, ordered actually, to appear at a gala event at Sam Roth's to celebrate a milestone for the studio, the release of its 1000th picture. Luckily, she and Simon had been prepared. Knowing they might have to attend a formal event they brought appropriate clothes. Although, looking at herself in the mirror now, Elizabeth felt a little uneasy.

She'd actually gone to the hotel salon and had her hair done. It was an extravagance, but the more they looked their parts, the more information people might be willing to share. And besides, it looked great. Back home, she was more of a wash and wear girl. She rarely got her hair done and, although it had taken forever and a day, she had to admit it looked wonderful. They'd smoothed it down and then set it into these perfect undulating waves. Add the dress and she barely recognized herself.

The dress was a bias-cut gown made from the most beautiful midnight blue silk satin. The top was shaped like a halter, the fabric clinging from the ribs to her knees and then flaring out in silky ripples. She looked in the mirror. It was slinky. *She* was slinky. She'd never been slinky before.

Simon came in to the bedroom dressed smartly in his single-breasted classic black tuxedo and swearing at his cufflinks. "I can't get these damn things on. Would you…?"

When he looked up, the rest of his sentence failed to materialize. His expression went from shocked to dark with desire and back to shocked in mere seconds.

"What…" He cleared his throat.

"Would you do me up?" She turned her back to him, facing the mirror again.

He looked at her reflection. His gaze drifted down her body, lingering over the areas where the dress left little to the imagination.

She tilted her head and swept her hair to the side to give him access to the not fully zipped zipper.

He broke away from staring at her and reached for the zipper. "Elizabeth," he said, his voice rough with desire and emotion. "You…" He said and then gently touched the bare skin just above her waist and ran his finger slowly up the contour of her spine. The shiver that followed his touch made her breath catch. "Aren't wearing…" His warm finger traced a circle between her shoulder blades.

"A bra?" she said surprised her brain could actually form a coherent thought.

He frowned and hmm'd in response.

"I'm not wearing underwear either," she said in a conspiratorial whisper. "Going commando."

She tried to make light of it. To be honest, she was feeling rather exposed and vulnerable. "Fashion dictates what fashion dictates," she said by way of explanation.

Simon's eyes found hers in the mirror. They were dark, almost angry. "Elizabeth…"

She couldn't tell if he was genuinely upset with her or not until his hands slid down to her waist and pulled her back against his body. Definitely not.

He bent down and whispered in her ear. "Stay here with me."

Now, it was Elizabeth's turn to lose her train of thought. Her mind was fuzzy and she felt more than a little dizzy. With one long finger, Simon eased her hair off her shoulder and kissed her neck. It was a feather light kiss and she felt the warmth of his breath as he whispered in her ear again. "Stay."

Elizabeth's eyes fluttered. It was wrong; they had to go. Despite those thoughts, she leaned her head back against his chest giving him better access. "Simon…"

He hmm'd again as he kissed his way down her neck to her collarbone.

"Alan," Elizabeth managed to say. "We need to go… to help Alan."

"Let him get his own girl," Simon said between kisses.

Elizabeth eased around in his arms and touched the edge of the bruise that still shone on his jaw. "It's important."

She could see the desire in his eyes, feel it in his body as it pressed against hers. The intensity in his expression was nearly overwhelming. He gently brushed her hair back from her face.

"If it were ever a choice between you and the world," he said, "the world would be damned."

Elizabeth pushed up onto her tiptoes and kissed him tenderly. When she pulled back the fierceness in his eyes had softened, but the fire of his passion for her never did. She left the comfort of his arms and walked to the doorway.

She tried to be as sultry as she felt and put one hand high on the doorframe. "We can pick this up wh—" She stopped and her hand fell down to her side. "What am I crazy?" She walked back over to him. "Just don't mess up my hair."

Simon laughed and pulled her to him. Alan and the rest of the world could wait.

ELIZABETH HAD THOUGHT ALAN'S mansion was impressive. It was a chicken coop compared to Sam Roth's. A long drive wound its way through manicured lawns up to the main house. The circular drive at the top of the hill was crowded with cars and limousines.

Simon helped Elizabeth out of the backseat and paid the driver. They fell in with the rest of the arrivals and walked across the gravel driveway to the front door.

A fully staffed coat check was set up in the foyer. Elizabeth let her wrap slip off her shoulders and handed it to one of the attendants.

"Won't you be cold?" Simon asked, his brow creased with concern that had nothing to do with her being cold.

"Don't be silly."

Simon sighed, accepted the ticket from the attendant and slipped it into his pocket. "This is going to be a long night."

Elizabeth shook her head and walked in ahead of him, with just a little extra sway in her hips. She could feel him watching her and heard him say softly, "A very long night."

The party was in full swing as they entered. The lower level of Roth's home was open and partygoers spilled into various rooms. A group of men played billiards and smoked cigars in one, while a raucous game of charades was going full bore in another. As they walked down the hall, a set of doors opened and she heard the telltale whirring and clicking of a movie projector coming from the darkened room. She glanced over just in time to see the credits start to roll against the screen. Like the MGM lion's roar, Mammoth Studios had its own logo, and a large wooly mammoth, well, a costumed elephant anyway, that reared and trumpeted. She heard the soft murmur of voices chattering before the film started as the doors to the room closed again.

They rounded a corner and entered the spacious main hall. A jazz quartet played soft standards as people helped themselves to canapés and champagne. Elizabeth spied Mr. Fox and Mr. Owl across the room and gave them a small wave. They mimed their eyes popping out like cartoon characters and raced across the room toward Simon and her.

"Hello, doll," Mr. Owl said.

"Mr. Doll," Mr. Fox added with a smile for Simon.

"You two look nice all cleaned up," Elizabeth said. Although, Mr. Owl's tuxedo was a little rumpled. She tried to smooth down one of his shoulder pads that insisted on popping up.

"That's not the suit," Mr. Fox said. "That's his hump. They're very close."

"Thank you, Master," Mr. Owl added in his best Igor impression.

"Has Grant arrived?" Simon asked, clearly hoping to interrupt their two-man show before it had a chance to move into the second act.

"I think I saw him back by the bar." Mr. Fox jerked his head toward another room.

Simon didn't waste any time and put his hand on Elizabeth's back and escorted her away. "Thank you."

Elizabeth turned as they walked away. "See you boys later?"

They both blew her kisses and then turned and blew each other kisses.

Despite the fact that waiters carried well-stocked trays of champagne around to the guests, the back room with the bar was packed with people. She and Simon tried to navigate through the crush, but it was too much.

"I'll see if I can find him," Simon offered.

Elizabeth gratefully let him swim upstream and filtered out into the hall to wait. Not a bad place to kill five minutes she thought as she noticed the artwork. The art on the walls should have been in a museum—a series of bas-relief bronzes by Matisse, a sketch by Picasso, and sculptures by Taft. It was an astonishing collection.

Elizabeth leaned in to get a better look at the Picasso.

"Beautiful, aren't they?"

She startled at the voice and turned quickly around.

Mr. Thorn smiled kindly at her. "I didn't mean to frighten you."

She swallowed and pushed her heart back into her chest. "It's all right. Yes, they are."

"It's a pity he has no idea what he has," Thorn said admiring the sketch. He caught her questioning eye and continued. "He knows their value, monetary value, but the beauty and passion of collecting is lost on a man like Roth."

Elizabeth moved down the hall to the Matisse. "Do you collect art too?"

"Not art," he said. "But I do enjoy collecting."

She could feel him looking at her and turned around. It was an odd sensation. It wasn't like when the other men looked at her. Those looks made her blush. This wasn't prurient although there was desire in his dark eyes.

He smiled and stepped closer. "I collect butterflies. A curious avocation for a man in my position, I suppose. Perhaps even distasteful?"

The idea should have offended her—the thought of the poor defenseless creatures pinned to a wall was instantly overridden by the sheer beauty of them. It was wrong, but they were so very beautiful.

He was standing close to her now. She could feel the power of his physical presence next to her. "Such delicate creatures," he said leaning down slightly. "The more beautiful they are the more difficult they are to find."

She found herself nodding, staring up at Thorn, a hazy sort of feeling making her brain gauzy.

"Elizabeth?"

"Hmm?"

She felt a hand grip her arm and turn her away from Thorn. Alan Grant stared down at her, angry and worried.

"We were looking for you," Elizabeth said, feeling the fog start to lift.

His expression faltered. "I'm sorry." He seemed to be apologizing for far more than being difficult to find, but she still couldn't think clearly. He shifted his gaze to Thorn, and his eyes that had been so tender a moment ago flashed with anger. "I told you to stay away from her."

Thorn was unimpressed. He put one hand casually in his pocket. "So you did."

Alan straightened his back and set his jaw. "Stay away."

Thorn smiled, but there was no humor or warmth in it. "It must be tempting. A simple trade."

Alan shook his head. "Never."

Thorn shrugged. "Well, should you change your mind, there's still time. Although," he added with a sad shake of his head, "Tick-tock, Alan, tick-tock."

What on earth were they talking about? Her mind was clearing, but the obvious history between the two men left her feeling like she'd missed a few important scenes in a movie.

"There you are!" a voice bellowed from the end of the hall. Sam Roth waved his cigar at Thorn. "Been looking for you."

Elizabeth felt relieved at Roth's sudden appearance, but she wasn't even sure why.

"Leo's here and he's feeling generous. Come on." Roth nodded toward Elizabeth and Grant in a cursory greeting.

Thorn turned to Elizabeth. "I'm sure we'll talk later." He smirked at Grant as he passed. "Grant."

He joined Roth at the end of the hall and they disappeared into the crowd.

"Are you all right?" Alan asked tipping Elizabeth's chin up to look into her eyes.

"I think so," she said. Her head was still a little swimmy. "I do have one question though." He looked at her expectantly. "What the *hell* was all that about?"

"Not here."

Elizabeth wanted to demand answers, but already her memory of the last few minutes was beginning to muddle.

Alan took her hand. "Come along, my dear Lucia."

He led her back into the main room where the Jazz quartet was playing "All of Me." Alan pulled her into the crowd and joined the dancers. "It's best if you pretend nothing happened." He took them into a graceful turn. "I'll explain everything later. Just try to avoid being alone with him, would you?"

Elizabeth didn't need to be reminded. The details of their encounter were fuzzy around the edges, but the heebies on her jeebies hadn't gone away. She would give Thorn a doublewide berth.

As the song ended and another began, she heard a throat clear behind her. She knew that cough. Simon.

He stood behind them, fists on hips, cranky on face.

Elizabeth looked up at him with a small smile and waved her hand in front of Grant. "Found him."

"So good of you to come tell me. I've been fighting that damn crowd for the last ten minutes looking for him. I—"

"I have just the thing to cure what ails you," Alan said and then maneuvered Elizabeth into Simon's arms, whose pique immediately started to ebb.

"I won't be far. We'll talk later," he added to Elizabeth. He started to leave and then turned back and addressed Simon, "Oh, and one more thing. Keep her away from Errol Flynn. Wandering hands." He looked Simon up and down and added. "Come to think of it, you might want to stay away from him too."

With that Alan slipped into the crowd.

After a beat to recover, Simon pulled Elizabeth to him and they started to dance.

"What was that all about?" he asked.

Elizabeth briefly considered telling Simon about her encounter with Thorn, but dismissed the idea immediately. Simon would not be happy and she wasn't honestly sure what to tell him. She trusted Alan could explain it better than she could. "I'm not sure. But, I think we'll find out soon."

BETTY WAS MURDER ON the clutch of her 1930 Model A, but she loved to drive. Despite the painful occasional grinding of gears, Jack was happy to sit back and watch her. She sat up straight and leaned toward the wheel, clearly loving every moment and the freedom of having her own car. It was an adventure each time, she'd said. And, as Jack gripped the edge of his seat as she sent them lurching through an intersection, he would have to agree.

"Most men want to drive," she said, turning to him with a smile.

He could see why, but he wouldn't have missed the look on her face for anything. "I'm not most men."

Her broadening smile said she agreed.

As much as he was enjoying the wild ride, he did have to wonder where they were going. After dinner, she'd asked if he was willing to get his feet wet. Not having the slightest idea what she meant, he'd readily agreed.

Now that they were speeding west toward the beach, he wondered just what she had in mind. It was past ten o'clock at night when they reached the Santa Monica bluffs not too far from the pier. They started down the long slope of the California Incline that would take them from the cliffs above to the long flat sandy shoreline. After a few more miles, she made a u-turn and parked along the ocean-side of the road.

"I think this is the place." She climbed out of the car and came around to the passenger side. He opened his door and waited. Just what did she have in mind?

She grinned playfully at him, steadied herself on the side of the car and started to take off her shoes. In his mind's eye, she didn't stop there. In reality she did. He looked at her curiously and she nodded toward his shoes. "Well...?"

He began to untie his shoes and take off his socks. "Are you going to tell me what we're doing or just toy with me?"

Betty simply arched an eyebrow in challenge. Jack laughed and put his shoes and socks inside the cab of the car and stepped out onto the sandy edge of the shore. Betty shook her head and knelt down at his feet. She rolled up his trouser legs to mid-calf and then stood back to admire her work.

"You might want to roll up your sleeves too."

He took off his jacket and undid his cuffs. She pulled a blanket from the backseat and held out her other hand to him.

"It's a little late for a picnic, isn't it?" he asked.

She just smiled, took his hand and led him out onto the beach. They trudged through the soft white sand, their feet slipping a half step for every step they made. The moon lit the shore ahead of them and Jack could just make out the silhouettes of a half dozen other people as they stood on a crest of sand above the shore's edge.

Suddenly, they disappeared and Betty yanked on his hand, urging him to hurry. "Come on!"

They quickened their pace and reached the end of the dry sand at the top of a small bank leading down to the water.

In the wet sand beneath them thousands of small, silver fish wiggled and flopped along the shore.

"Grunion!" Betty said. "I've always wanted to see this."

People ran in and out of the lapping waves as more fish came and then were pulled back out to sea. Some people had buckets and some gunnysacks and tried to scoop up handfuls of the fish as they washed on shore.

Jack had heard about grunion runs before, but he'd never seen one. The fish came on shore to spawn at high tide for several nights after the full moon. They wriggled up the beach as far as they could and then back out to sea. Some people stood by with flashlights while others tried to capture as many fish as they could. Grunion were small, maybe six inches long, but supposedly made for good cooking. The buckets full of fish some of the men caught would feed their family.

Betty tossed their blanket onto the dry sand and started down the small hill, her laughter caught in the cool ocean breeze. Tiptoeing along the edge of the gentle breakers, she tried not to step on any fish. She bent down to try to grab one, but they kept slipping through her fingers. She laughed and waved for him to join her.

The fish had long silver streaks along their sides and bellies that reflected the moonlight. They flipped and wiggled in a huge mass along the sand as far up the coast as they could see. Each wave washed some away and the next brought more to shore.

Betty giggled as the fish danced at her feet. She turned to face the water and the wind lifted her hair back and the moonlight touched her face. She was breathless and beautiful.

"Amazing, isn't it?" she said turning back to face him.

Cold waves lapped at his feet and Jack felt a burning in his chest. "Yes," he managed to say. "Amazing."

She smiled at him again and then turned away to chase the fish. Jack watched her for a moment and then joined the fray. He scooped one up and held it aloft triumphant. "Got one!"

She looked back and it squirted out of his hand. He tried vainly to chase after it. Betty laughed and then screamed as a large wave came and splashed them both. They waded in and out on the edge of the frenzy before walking back up the small hill and huddling together on the blanket. Before long someone had built a large bonfire in the middle of the broad expanse of dry sand. People made their way to it and sat down to warm themselves against the night.

Jack felt Betty shiver next to him. "Come on," he said, nodding toward the fire.

He stood and held out a hand to her. Her cool fingers slipped in his and he helped her stand. When they reached the group by the fire, Jack asked if they could sit and dry their clothes. The man, who didn't speak any English said something in Spanish and then just smiled and gestured to a spot by the fire.

Jack put the blanket down and rested his back against a large log. Betty leaned into him for warmth and he pulled her close to his side. They listened to the crackling of the fire and the waves breaking in the distance. It was so quiet and calm and felt slightly surreal after the manic excitement by the water.

Jack took both of Betty's hands, so small and chilled, between his own, rubbed them gently and blew on them softly. "Still cold?" he asked after a few minutes.

She shrugged and shook her head, but he could tell she was. "Here," he said as he gently maneuvered her to sit between his legs and lean back against his chest. He flipped the end of the blanket up over her exposed legs and wrapped his arms around her middle.

"Better?"

He felt her nod against his chest and he wondered if she could feel the pounding of his heart. One of her hands came to rest on his thigh. He put his hand over hers and wished it could always be like this.

The fire blazed on into the night and the long shadows danced on the sand. A bottle of something made the rounds a few times and one of the men took out his guitar and played a series of classical Spanish songs Jack had never heard before.

Betty nuzzled into his warmth and he let his lips graze the crown of her head. How long they stayed that way, content to just be in each other's arms, Jack couldn't say, but he knew nothing so perfect could last forever.

He did everything in his power to delay the end of their evening, but the hours passed and the night grew late. The fire burned down low and slowly everyone made their way back to their cars and their homes and the reality of tomorrow.

Jack held her hand as they walked up the path to her house. He looked down at their hands, twined together and wondered how he'd ever be able to let go.

They walked up the few steps to the small landing at her front door. Reluctantly, he let go of her hand. She dug into her purse, found the key and unlocked the door. She pushed it open, but then paused and turned around to face him. The yellow glass from the porch light made her pale skin a warm, golden color. The glow from the streetlamp behind him caught in her eyes and looked like starlight. Jack was never at a loss for words until now. She literally took his breath away.

Her eyes traveled over his face, dipping down to his mouth, which had suddenly gone dry, and then her gaze fell shyly to the ground between them. "I guess this is goodnight," she said.

"Yeah." His voice was husky and soft. And he was an idiot. Say something, idiot. "I..."

She looked up at him, unsure and nervous. "You..."

"I had a great time," he said. Complete idiot.

She smiled, relieved at having something concrete to respond to. "I did too. It was..."

"Yeah," he said again. He'd never had a problem talking to women before. Why on earth did he feel like this now? Like his limbs were attached to some else's body.

"Aw hell," he said and took a long stride that closed the gap between them. Before she could react, he grabbed her arm with one hand and slid his other behind her head and pulled her to him and kissed her.

He caught her mouth in a surprised little "oh" and nearly stopped. He felt her hands grip the fabric of his shirt, but she didn't push him away; she pulled him closer. And he was lost.

He poured everything he couldn't say into that one kiss. When finally, she pulled back he was breathing heavily and happy to see she was too. He caught his breath and slowly released her, hoping he hadn't gone too far.

She looked down again, afraid to meet his eyes. Her fingers untwined from the fists they'd made in his shirt. Nervously, still half dazed, she touched the corner of her mouth. When their eyes met again, it took all of his self-control not to take her in another kiss. But he'd be damned if he was going to screw this up.

"I should go," he said.

She looked at him, that same shy unsure beautiful light in her eyes. She bit her lower lip and he nearly reached out to her.

Betty ducked her head and stepped back into the open doorway, disappearing into the darkness for a moment before turning back to him. She rested her head against the door jam, her hand playing with the edge of the molding. "Or," she said, her eyes catching his briefly. "You could stay."

He knew he shouldn't. "Maybe," he said, taking a step closer and looking into her eyes. "Just for a little while."

She stepped back into the darkness and her door opened further inviting him in; he could do nothing else and stepped into the darkness with her.

Chapter Twelve

SIMON WAS GROWING IMPATIENT. Whatever secret Grant and Elizabeth shared started to eat away at him. He'd endured banal conversation and feigned an interest in a half-dozen people he wouldn't remember in the morning for long enough.

He went to collect them and demand that they tell him what was going on. The two of them were off to the side by the hall, laughing and drinking as if there was nothing wrong in the least.

"I think it's time we leave," Simon started, "and you—"

Simon was interrupted by a slight commotion a few feet away. A young man, who couldn't have been more than seventeen, barged into the room. He was sorely out of place. His suit was brown and wrinkled and far too big for him. He mumbled an apology and tugged at his collar. He ran a dirty hand through the fringe of his hair as his eyes darted around the room, searching for someone.

The young man's eyes went wide as he seemed to find whom he was searching for. Simon followed his gaze. Sam Roth.

"Trouble?" Alan asked.

Roth hadn't noticed and casually ended a conversation with someone, excused himself and exited into the hall. The young man's chest rose and fell quickly with fear and adrenaline. He shoved one hand deeply into his jacket pocket, hunched his shoulders and followed.

"I'm afraid so," Simon finally answered. "Elizabeth, please don't—"

He turned around to ask her not to get involved, but she was already following the young man and Roth from the room. She turned back and waved for them to follow. Simon swore under his breath and ignored Grant's delighted laugh.

They caught up with Elizabeth at the entrance to the main hallway. The boy looked around nervously and nearly caught them staring right at him.

"Don't talk to me about the Academy!" Grant said suddenly. "Laughton is a hack!" He spun around, his back to the boy now, and nearly bumped into one of Roth's prized statues as he stood sloppily in front of Simon and Elizabeth.

It took Simon a moment to realize what Grant was doing. "A travesty," Simon said loudly joining Grant's argument mid-flow.

Grant thumped Simon on the chest in agreement. "I could have played Henry the VIII *and* two of his wives with both hands tied behind my back!"

Simon could see the boy dart into a room and nodded to Alan who stopped swaying and fell in with them. The trio continued down the hall.

"I love Charles Laughton," Elizabeth said softly.

"Traitor."

They inched down the hall and came to the door the boy had gone through. Thankfully, he'd been in such a rush, he hadn't closed it behind him. Inside the study, Sam Roth stood, hands in the air and a dark scowl on his face. The boy held a revolver leveled at Roth's chest.

His hand trembled and his finger inched closer to the trigger. "She was my sister."

"Take it easy, kid," Roth said, trying to inch closer to his desk. "Who was your sister?"

"Sara!" The boy took a stuttering step closer. "Sara Brown!"

"I don't know her. You're mixed up. Look, kid—"

"No." The boy shook his head. "No, she was mixed up. And you did it to her."

Roth shook his head and then noticed the trio at the doorway. His eyes went wide and the boy spun around, following his gaze.

Simon's heart raced and he started to step in front of Elizabeth to shield her.

"Stop!" the boy yelled. He spun back and forth between Roth and the door. "Get in," he said, waving the gun at them. "Shut it."

The three of them slowly made their way around the perimeter of the study until they were near Sam Roth.

The boy was breathing hard now, caught between panic and anger. "You were part of it, weren't you?"

"Listen son," Roth said.

Tears were streaming down the boy's face. "I am not your son. I was *her* brother. And you and your lies, they killed her."

"Ruby?" Elizabeth said.

The boy's attention and the gun he held moved toward her. Simon's hand inched closer to Elizabeth's arm, ready to snatch her from the line of fire.

The boy's face crumpled for a moment. His expression held such a look of pain and sorrow Simon was struck by the force of it. "That's what they turned her into."

"I'm sorry about your sister, kid, but—" Sam said.

"Shut up!" The boy turned his attention back to Sam, but he was growing more panicky and more dangerous by the minute. "That's not what he said. He said you tricked her. You turned her into something she wasn't. You killed her."

Out of the corner of his eye, Simon saw Elizabeth take a step closer to Roth. He groaned inwardly. Damn it, what was she doing? She raised her hands in front her showing she was no threat. Simon wanted to grab her and pull her back to his side, but any movement might set the boy off.

"What's your name?" she asked.

"What does it..." he started, but a woman's presence and her soothing voice seemed to get through to him. "Walter."

"This isn't what...Sara would have wanted, is it, Walter?"

Walter seemed to be wavering, but his finger was still on the trigger and the gun was still pointed at Roth, and damned if Elizabeth wasn't standing at his side now.

"She wouldn't want you to hurt anyone or get yourself hurt, would she, Walter?"

She was getting through to him now. Simon could see the doubt clouding his eyes.

"Yeah, kid," Roth said. "Don't be stupid."

As soon as Roth spoke the words, Simon knew it had been a mistake. Walter's expression changed in an instant. His hand stilled and his face hardened.

"You sonofa—"

Simon lunged forward, knowing he was too far away, knowing he'd be too late. As he leapt forward, something flew past his head and struck Walter's arm just as the gun fired. The puff of smoke lingered in the air as the gun fell out of the boy's grip just as Simon collided with him. They landed in a tangled heap on the floor.

The boy cried out with pain and gripped his forearm with his free hand.

"Elizabeth!"

Simon pushed off the boy and kicked the gun across the room. Grant picked it up and Simon hurried over to Elizabeth. She and Roth had fallen back onto his desk.

"Are you hurt?" Simon asked, reaching out to her.

"I'm okay."

Simon let out a fast breath and turned to Roth who nodded that he was all right too. Simon helped him stand. The bullet hole in the portrait of Roth behind the desk was silent testament to how close they'd come.

"Everyone all right?" Grant asked as he stood over the boy, gun in one hand. He bent down and picked up the golden Oscar statuette from the ground at his feet. "Charles Laughton, my ass."

Walter seemed to be in a state of shock and sat quietly, head down, cradling his injured arm. Grant helped him into a chair and sat down opposite him and lit a cigarette. Partygoers who'd heard the shot hurried into the study. Some offered genuine concern, but it seemed most were merely concerned with making sure they were part of a story sure to be front-page news tomorrow.

Sam Roth's wife, an attractive middle-aged woman with graying hair and too many strands of pearls, fluttered in. She was in quite a state, despite Roth's repeated assurances that he was fine. At Roth's urging a couple helped his wife from the room and promised to look after her. Just as Roth had managed to sweep the room clear again, two blasted photographers even managed to get off a few quick shots before he slammed the study door in their faces.

Simon could hardly care about any of that, about any of them. He was focused on Elizabeth, his brave and deranged wife, who stood safe and at his side. Her cheeks were still flushed with the blush of adrenaline. It was deeply bothersome that she positively glowed after nearly being killed and even more troubling that he'd seen her in that state more than once.

"Are you sure you're not hurt?" he asked again.

She sighed and then smoothed down her dress. Her eyes went wide in alarm. "Oh no."

Simon's heart seized in his chest. "What's wrong?"

She wrinkled her nose and turned her hip to the side. "I ripped it."

"Elizabeth," Simon breathed. He really needed to take up jogging again. His heart couldn't take much more of this.

The police arrived a few minutes later and as they were escorting Walter out of the room, Benny Roth arrived. It could have been Simon's imagination, but something seemed to pass between the two men. It was difficult to say though as Benny hurried to his brother's side. It seemed that Walter was hardly in his right mind, but Simon filed away the incident nonetheless.

"Nice of you to show," Sam said to his brother.

"I got caught up with things." He looked at the bullet hole that tore through the midsection of the portrait behind the desk. "Close call."

"Too close. Be dead if it weren't for them. Comedy writers. Finally good for something," he said with a smirk, but his gratitude bled through the casual comment.

Benny Roth gave them both a quick once over and walked over to Simon. "Have we met? You look familiar."

"You probably saw us at the studio," Elizabeth said.

"Yeah, I guess that's it," Benny said. Sam Roth made quick introductions.

Benny's expression was tight, forced. Perhaps he was just upset about nearly losing his brother. "I suppose I should thank you." He stuck out his hand for Simon to shake. "For saving my brother's life."

Simon shook it. "We just happened to be in the right place at the right time."

Benny nodded thoughtfully.

There was a knock on the study door and two police officers entered. "We know you've been through a lot, but we've gotta get statements."

Benny Roth turned to his brother. "I'll go check on Midge."

Sam nodded his thanks and Benny Roth slipped between the officers and out the door. The officer with the ruddy, pockmarked face took off his cap and approached Simon and Elizabeth. "I'll try not to keep ya too long."

The questions were cursory and routine. They seemed to have made up their mind before the investigation had even started. Walter Brown was an angry young man, avenging what he saw as the murder of his beloved sister.

"He did say something about a 'him'," Elizabeth said. "Remember, Simon? He said something like 'he said you'd say that' or something."

The officer scribbled something in his notebook. "Any idea who this 'him' is?"

"No," Elizabeth said.

"You?" the officer asked Simon.

Simon remembered the exchanged glance between Benny Roth and the boy. Roth certainly had something to gain from his brother's death, but…"No," Simon said. "No idea, I'm afraid."

The officer stared at Simon for a long moment and then nodded. "Thanks." He glanced at his notes. "You be at the Ambassador for a few more days?"

"Yes," Elizabeth said.

"Good," the officer said with a smile. "We'll be in touch."

Strangely, an attempted murder hadn't put an end to the party. If anything, it seemed to have re-energized it. However, Simon had had his fill and convinced Grant and Elizabeth it was time to leave. He hadn't forgotten their earlier secret, and waited impatiently for them to offer it up on the drive to Grant's home.

It wasn't until they were safely tucked away from the world in Grant's living room that Simon reached his limit. "What happened earlier?"

Elizabeth flopped down onto the sofa and kicked off her shoes. "Attempted murder, mayhem, a little dancing."

Grant made a tray of drinks and started toward the coffee table.

Simon was not amused. "Earlier. What happened earlier when I went in search of Grant?"

Grant doubled back and added a full bottle of scotch to the tray, paused and then added another.

Elizabeth stopped massaging her feet, tucked them up under her and settled deep into the sofa cushions. She frowned and rubbed her arm in thought. "I'm not sure."

"That's not an answer," Simon said. "Elizabeth—"

"Don't be too hard on her," Grant said as he set down the tray and offered Simon a drink. Simon took the glass, but placed it untouched on the side table next to the sofa. "Thorn has that effect on people."

"Thorn." Just the mere mention of the man's name made Simon tense. "What did he do?"

Elizabeth shook her head. "Nothing. I think. I was in the hall waiting for you and then he was just there."

"He materialized out of nowhere?" Simon asked.

Elizabeth gave him a sour look. "No. He came up behind me and was admiring the art."

"I'm sure," Simon said as he paced behind the side chair adjacent to the sofa. He felt an irrational surge of jealousy and pushed it aside.

If Elizabeth noticed his reaction, she ignored it. "And then Alan was there, and…"

Grant took the seat opposite Simon's chair.

"And…" Simon prompted.

"I'm not sure," Elizabeth said with a frown and looked helplessly to Grant.

"And?" Simon said to him, patience wearing very thin now.

"And I think you'd better sit down."

Why was it people said that? Was it supposed to somehow soften the blow? All it managed to do was heighten Simon's already pulsating anxiety. In lieu of strangling the truth out of everyone in the room, he forced himself to sit down and gestured for Grant to continue.

"And your drink," Grant said. "You might want—"

"What I want," Simon said angrily, "is to know what the bloody hell is going on!"

"Simon…"

"No," Grant said, "I don't blame him. He has every right." He leaned back in his chair and stared into the bottom of his glass before speaking. "Edgar Thorn is an…unusual man. People often feel the way Elizabeth does right now, confused and unsure, after an encounter."

Simon frowned. "Encounter? That's an odd choice of words."

"Is it? Edgar Thorn is an odd sort of man. Or no man at all."

"What is it you're not saying, Mr. Grant?" Simon asked with far more patience than he had or Grant deserved.

Grant pondered the question for a moment and then nodded, seemingly coming to some sort of conclusion. "What I'm about to tell you will sound absurd, even insane perhaps, but I assure you, I believe it with all my heart."

He stood and walked over to a bookcase, scanning the shelves briefly before pulling down an old leather-bound volume. Grant pushed out a breath and carried the book over to Simon.

"Are you familiar with the story of Faust?" he said as he held it out to him.

Simon looked at the book—Christopher Marlowe's *The Tragicall History of the Life and Death of Doctor Faustus.* "In the play, a German scholar, dissatisfied with the limits of knowledge, of his life, learns the black arts and summons Mephistopheles, a messenger for the Devil. Faustus offers Satan a bargain. In exchange for, I think it was 24 years of knowledge and power, Faustus will give the Devil—"

"His soul," Grant finished for him.

"It's an ancient legend," Simon said. "It predates Marlowe by several hundred years, perhaps more. From Paganini to military generals, people have claimed a deal with the devil has given them special powers or used it to justify witch hunts."

Grant arched an eyebrow. "You're quite knowledgeable on the topic."

Simon put the book aside. "I'm an academic. I've studied things like this for many years. But I fail to see what this has to do with Thorn."

"Seven years ago, I was playing Richard the III in Poughkeepsie," Grant said as he walked over to stand in front of a fireless hearth. "Of course, back then I was Alan Krueger." He turned to face them, arms out at his sides. "Everything about me is a lie. I was born in New Jersey, for God's sake."

"What happened in Poughkeepsie?" Simon asked, hoping to keep Grant from falling off the rails completely.

"Nothing," Grant said. "Nothing *ever* happens in Poughkeepsie." He walked back over to his chair, but didn't sit. "And so, like every wide-eyed idiot, I came to Hollywood to seek my fame and fortune. And I was cast as 'Man Dying of Scurvy' in the *Sea Beast*. Fame and fortune seemed very far away. Until I met—"

"Thorn," Elizabeth said.

Grant nodded. "He was very persuasive. I thought he was joking at first, of course, but he had a way about him. As though he could see inside you and move the pieces around."

"Yes," Simon said, remembering how he'd felt upon meeting Thorn. "But surely, you're not suggesting Thorn is some sort of Mephistopheles."

"No." Grant sank down into his chair. "I think," he said, leaning back. "He's the Devil himself."

Simon shook his head slowly. "You'll forgive me, but that seems a bit of a stretch."

"It's absurd, isn't it?" Grant said. "And yet. After I signed my contract, everything I'd wished for came true. I'd spent years trying to do what he accomplished for me in the blink of an eye."

"He's a man with a lot of power at the studio, isn't he?" Elizabeth said. "He didn't need any supernatural help to create a career for you."

"I told myself that at first. But then as I saw what he did for…to other people, I began to doubt."

"People like Ruby?" Elizabeth said.

"Yes."

Simon shook his head. "That's hardly evidence of a demonic presence on the earthly plane. Thorn is a powerful manipulator," Simon said, "But beyond that…"

Grant shed his coat and unbuttoned his shirtsleeve. "After I signed the contract, this appeared the next morning." He rolled his sleeve up to his bicep, took his handkerchief out and rubbed at the inner crease of his elbow. Once the covering make-up was gone, a small, raised bluish mark took shape. He sat forward and presented it for them to see.

Elizabeth moved closer to get a better look. "The Devil's mark."

Grant nodded. "We all have them."

Simon was still far from convinced. Natural explanations far outstripped the supernatural ones at this point, although, it would be foolish to dismiss any possibility out of hand quite yet. He moved to sit next to Elizabeth and reached out to touch the scar. Grant pulled back. "I'm not afraid of it," Simon said.

"You should be."

"Devil's mark or not, it's not contagious." He felt along the skin. "Slightly raised, some sort of brand." Simon leaned back into the cushions. "That's hardly proof. Something like that can be produced with conventional means. A small branding iron."

Grant rolled down his sleeve. "I think I'd remember that."

"Yes, but Thorn is a master manipulator. Perhaps, he uses drugs somehow to magnify his powers of persuasion."

Simon ticked off a list of potential causal agents in his mind, discarding most as quickly as he thought of them.

"Wait a minute," Elizabeth said. "You said, 'We all have them.'"

"Yes, that poor girl Ruby, Benny Roth and at least two other men who are already dead."

"Benny Roth too?" Elizabeth said, putting the pieces together. "And Sam Roth?"

Grant shook his head. "Not that I know of. The rest of us, you see, we all 'met' Thorn around the same time."

"That dinner at Musso & Frank..." Elizabeth said.

"A last supper of sorts," Grant said with a bitter laugh.

Simon heard the fear and resignation in Grant's voice. Belief was half the battle. If Thorn had Grant convinced of his fate and Grant wasn't willing to fight for his own life, was Simon really ready to risk his own and Elizabeth's for him?

"Do you want to live?" Simon asked Grant.

The question caught him off guard. "Of course, I do. Doesn't—"

"We're willing to fight, however we can to help you, but if you don't—

"I told you," Grant said impatiently. "There's nothing you can do for me, but you're missing the point entirely. That's not why I am worried."

"No?" Simon was skeptical of that.

"Of course, I'd rather not forfeit my soul, but there's something else. When I interrupted Thorn and Elizabeth earlier this evening, he reminded me of…an option."

"That sounds promising," Elizabeth said.

Simon didn't share her enthusiasm. Historically, the options for such things were seldom favorable. Suddenly, he had a horrible cold as iron feeling in the pit of his stomach.

Grant's expression grew dark. "A soul that has been bargained for can be retrieved if a purer soul, one that's unsullied, is given in exchange."

"In several versions of the legend, a fair maiden does offer herself," Simon said.

"In Hollywood, fair maidens are the legends." He looked at Elizabeth. "Present company excepted, I'm afraid."

"Me? I'm not a maiden," she said. "I'm not a virgin. We do it all the time."

Grant had the good sense to let that remark go. "My dear, it's not that part of you that he's interested in."

"It's your soul," Simon said.

CHAPTER THIRTEEN

SIMON SET HIS CUFFLINKS down on top of the dresser and walked silently over to the overstuffed chair by the small table in their hotel bedroom. He'd been simmering since they'd left Grant's, and judging from his body language, he was ready to come to a full boil any time now.

He looked at her through narrowed eyes as he tugged at one end of his bowtie. He loosened the knot and let the black ends of silk fall onto his chest. Elizabeth winced. She knew that look. That was the *Dear God in Heaven, Woman, what have you gotten us into now?* look. Which, honestly, she only half-deserved. Maybe three-quarters. But, Elizabeth also knew Simon's anger wasn't really directed at her all. He hated not being in control of things, and he hated her being in danger most of all.

She braced herself for his opening salvo, but Simon just sighed heavily and sat down in the chair. He undid the top button on the collar of his shirt, still looking at her intently. Finally, he shook his head, leaned forward and loosened the laces to his dress shoes. Maybe he was going to have the whole argument with himself and leave her out of it completely?

"Ridiculous," he said under his breath.

Or not.

He sat up in the chair, toed off his shoes and fixed her again with his most quelling glare. If she'd been a first year and not his wife, she would have scurried away like a rabbit. But, she knew the man behind the façade now and deep down, he knew she was right. That staying was right. He just needed to wander in the wilderness a little while first.

"I didn't do it on purpose, you know?" she said.

Simon leaned back in his chair and crossed one long leg over the other, his ankle resting on his knee. He arched an eyebrow and tugged off his sock. "Drawing the attention of the Devil or almost getting shot?"

Ouch. "Uhm, the first part?"

Simon hmm'd and switched legs.

Elizabeth looked down at the rip in the side of her beautiful dress and poked a finger through the hole. This was why she shouldn't have nice things.

Simon tossed his sock aside, put his bare feet on the floor and curled his hands around the front ends of the arm rests. He looked like a king on his throne, a damn sexy king, waiting for her to continue.

"I seem to remember," Elizabeth said, "that I wasn't alone creeping down the hall after the armed man."

"I don't creep."

She saw the fleeting smile tug at the corner of his mouth. "You know what I mean," she said. "We saw someone in trouble and we helped him." She pointed at Simon and herself. "*We* helped him."

"Yes, but this is different." He stood and untucked his dress shirt from his pants.

"You don't really think he's the Devil, do you?"

Simon paused and thought for a moment. "I'm not sure." He unbuttoned his shirt as he thought aloud. "Considering the things we've seen in our travels, it's not irrational to consider some sort of spirit or demon could be at work. But, a sociopath like Rasputin or Crowley seems far more likely. And hardly any more comforting a thought."

Despite his words to the contrary, Elizabeth did find the thought an odd relief. She'd seen the demon in King Kashian's eyes and felt something…unnatural in San Francisco. She'd rather fight flesh and blood any day. Simon might still harbor a healthy skepticism, but she didn't. The unlikely grew more likely with everything she'd seen.

"Regardless," Simon said, "devil, demon or sociopath; Thorn is dangerous. And the idea that he's focusing his attention on you…"

She could see the muscles in jaw working as he shook his head. "Unacceptable."

She couldn't argue with that.

Simon must have taken her silence as acquiescence because he stood a little taller and said, "I'll call Jack in the morning."

"Invite him for lunch at the Derby."

"That isn't what I meant."

Elizabeth smiled. "I know, but we can't leave. Not yet."

"Grant himself said there's nothing we can do to help. Staying here, putting you in danger, is an unnecessary risk."

"We don't know there's nothing we can do and I think it's necessary." She met him at the foot of the bed and turned around, silently asking him to unzip her and, hopefully, listen.

Simon undid her dress and she took a few steps away.

"It's too dangerous," he said simply.

Elizabeth slipped the dress over her hips and stepped out of it. She laid it gently on the edge of the bed and turned to him. "It's—"

Simon waved a hand to stop her. "If we're going to argue, you can't be naked." His eyes raked over her bare body. "I need my higher brain...something, and that..." he said gesturing with a sigh at her and losing his thought. His jaw clenched. "Elizabeth..."

"All right." She retrieved their folded pajamas from the dresser drawer and heard Simon grunt in appreciation, as she turned away and bent over to get into them. She grinned demurely as she stood and tossed the bottoms across the room. They hit him in the chest and fell onto the bed between them.

Elizabeth pulled on the pajama top and lifted her arms as if to say, *is this better?*

"Thank you," he said, as he shed his shirt and unbuttoned his trousers.

Elizabeth caught sight of his long, muscular thighs before having the sense to look away. "We still have three days until the contract runs out. And, it's not like this is a case of demon possession. Alan even said that the whole deal has to be voluntary. Thorn doesn't oogie-boogie and jump out like a soul snatching snatcher-person."

Out of the corner of her eye, she saw Simon straighten up and begin to tie the pajama string. "Yes, but if there's truly nothing we can do—"

"We don't know that. Alan's frightened, but he's a man." She ignored Simon's sour expression and pressed on. "He isn't used to asking for help. And besides, you don't help someone because they ask you to; you help someone because they need it."

Simon had no reply to that. He walked into the bathroom and turned on the taps. "Don't forget Benny Roth. He's part of this too and, perhaps, just as dangerous."

Elizabeth followed him into the bath and washed her face as they talked. "Do you really think he was behind the attempt on his brother's life?"

"It's possible. I doubt he hired the boy, but there was definitely a connection between the two. At the very least, I think he encouraged it. The boy was genuinely upset, no doubt of that, but it was equally clear that he was far out of his depth. From his clothes and his accent, I'd guess a farmer, Midwest probably." Simon handed her a towel. "And poor. How did he get the money for the train ticket? How did he know where to find Sam?"

"I hadn't thought of that. Poor kid," she said. "If Benny needed money and Sam wouldn't give it to him, killing him would be one way to get it."

Simon nodded, leaned toward the mirror and touched the nearly-healed abrasion and bruise on his chin.

"Does it still hurt?" Elizabeth asked.

"No, but it does serve as a reminder."

"That you should lead with your left?"

Simon smiled tightly. "No," he said drawing out the word. He squirted a blob of toothpaste onto his toothbrush and handed the tube to her. "That being here is dangerous and has consequences."

"We knew there would be risks. Sebastian's list, his unfinished missions, there's danger built in, but people need our help."

She stuck her toothbrush in her mouth and started to scrub. Simon frowned and followed suit. They glared at each other over their toothbrushes. Eventually, Simon finished first and leaned over the sink to rinse. Elizabeth wasn't finished though and kept brushing. She could see it was making him impatient, which just made her brush that much longer.

"Spit," he said. And when she smiled at him with a frothy, cheeky grin, he pointed at the sink. "In there."

Elizabeth rinsed her mouth and the argument picked up where it left off. "When we agreed to come here," she said, "we accepted the risks."

Simon shut off the light in the bath as they re-entered the bedroom.

"Risk, yes, but not every risk." Simon walked around to his side of the bed and waited for her to get under the covers before turning off the light and joining her.

"We knew it wouldn't be easy," she said to the darkness.

Simon lay on his back and sighed. Elizabeth pushed herself up on an elbow and watched his face in the moonlight.

"It will never be *easy* for me to put you in danger."

His head rolled to the side and Elizabeth leaned in to kiss him. He pulled her into his arms and she shifted so that her head was resting on his chest.

"Someone needs our help," she said. "The watch, the list. It's what we're meant to do. It's who we are now."

Simon traced the contours of her check with the tips of his fingers. "Tomorrow," he said, his voice deep and husky. "We'll be those people tomorrow. Tonight, I just want to be a man who's lucky enough to be sharing a bed with his beautiful wife."

JACK POURED HIMSELF A cup of coffee and tried not to make a sound as he pulled his chair out from under the small table in Betty's kitchen. He started to take a sip, but could feel the heat against his lips as it drew closer. He blew on it a few times and set it aside to let it cool. Finally, he pushed it away.

He'd woken up in plenty of women's beds in his life and usually the last thing on his mind was a hot cup of coffee. And yet, here he was—waiting and worrying. Why had he eased his arms away from around Betty's warm body and slipped out of bed unseen? Why hadn't he kissed her shoulder and woken her in the early morning to make love again when sleep had given up on him? Why was he sitting here alone?

He tried to distract himself from those questions by looking for something to eat, but his heart wasn't in it. His heart was still in bed with her. Why wasn't he?

The answer was plain and painful in the cold light of day. He'd been such a fool, a fool for love, but a fool nonetheless. He wanted her. He wanted her so badly; he'd ignored everything but her. He'd ignored the warning bells that rang like air raid sirens now.

He'd had plenty of relationships built on lies; maybe they all had been in a way. But now that he wanted to tell the truth, to be completely honest with someone, he couldn't. What could he see say? *Hello, I'm from the future. Let's go to Carmel for the weekend?*

It was impossible.

Could he stay? Could she go? What would any of that mean for the timeline? For them?

"Good morning," a soft voice said from behind him.

He turned and saw Betty looking more beautiful than any woman had a right to. She smiled shyly at him and wrapped her robe more tightly about her waist. Jack stood and kissed her lightly. She laughed and pulled him in for another, deeper kiss.

His body responded as it had last night, all night.

She eased out of his arms. "Hungry?"

"Starved."

She opened a small milk door, a little opening to a cubbyhole in the wall of the house for deliveries, and pulled out a fresh pint of milk. "I think I have some eggs."

He nodded and she put the milk on the counter. "Good, and then maybe we can talk," Betty said. Jack felt his stomach clench at that. He didn't want to talk. He didn't want to keep lying. She turned around and a blush stole across her cheeks. "I don't really know anything about you."

"I'm an open book," he lied and hated the way it tasted in his mouth. "Ask me anything."

"Well," she said nervously. "Where are you from?"

"Texas originally." The lies came naturally. He'd been telling them for far too long. "But I've lived lots of places. Chicago, Nevada."

"Any family?"

"Kid sister," Jack said, thinking of Elizabeth. "And her husband, I guess, too."

"You don't like him?"

"I do actually. It's just more fun if he doesn't know that." At least that part wasn't a lie.

She laughed and then suddenly stopped. "What time is it? Would you get the paper?" she asked. "If I leave it out past eight, Mrs. Geary across the street steals it."

"Sure," Jack said.

Taking a last sip of his coffee, he went to the front door, glad to escape her questions and feeling guilty for the thought. He took a deep breath of fresh morning air and looked out at the sleepy neighborhood. What the hell was he doing? He had his second chance and it was practically perfect. And yet, he felt it all slipping away. He'd been supposed to keep to himself, keep a low profile. So much for that, he thought, as he waved and smiled to a rather shocked woman across the street who wrapped her robe tightly about her and ducked back into her house.

Jack sighed and found the paper resting on the second step. As he picked it up, he unfolded it. Emblazoned on the front page was a picture of Sam Roth and Alan Grant with Simon and Elizabeth in the background. The headline read: Attempted Murder, Foiled by Star & Others.

"So much for a low-profile."

CHAPTER FOURTEEN

THE TAXI WOUND ITS way up through the hills of Los Feliz, a small affluent community east of Hollywood and just touching the southern edge of Griffith Park. Rugged, chaparral and sage-covered slopes mixed with tall oaks and Manzanita pines.

While Simon's knowledge of the occult was impressive and Elizabeth's wasn't too shabby either, both of them felt the reflexive need to research their problem. They'd checked in with Jack that morning, assuring him they were fine and telling him about their evening with Alan Grant.

Simon gave Jack the highlights of Alan's revelation of his pact with Thorn and his suspicions about Benny Roth's involvement in Sam's attempted murder. They asked him if he could find a connection between Roth and the boy. It probably won't help them, but it might help the kid. They arranged to meet Jack for dinner that night at the Brown Derby and exchange notes. That left Simon and Elizabeth free to research.

If they were going to find a way to help Alan, they needed to know more about his agreement with Thorn. While the Los Angeles public library was pretty impressive it was shockingly low on information about deals with the devil. For that, they needed a repository of esoteric knowledge. Luckily, Los Angeles was lousy with them. As it was in the future, Los Angeles attracted the oddball, the seeker, the alternative life-styler.

Religious and philosophical outcasts had been making Los Angeles their home for the last ten to twenty years. The hills outside the city had housed Theosophical compounds and retreats of every imaginable variety. The trick was getting access. Not surprisingly, most of them relished their privacy and were wary of strangers. The one major exception was Manly Hall. Hall was an author, speaker and world-renowned mystic.

They were headed for his soon-to-be opened Philosophical Research Society. The society itself hadn't been founded yet, but the research materials were bound to be there. Or at least, they hoped they were. Manly Hall had spent the last few years traveling Europe and acquiring the preeminent collection of religious, occult and esoteric texts in the world. If anyone had material about a pact with the devil, it was Hall.

"This isn't right." Simon leaned forward and instructed the cabbie on where he'd gone wrong and they turned around and started back down the hill. They passed Frank Lloyd Wright's Ennis House, an enormous building that looked something like a Mayan temple.

"Curious, isn't it?" Simon said. "Modern architecture that imitates an ancient culture."

Elizabeth peered out of the cab window. "What's old is new again."

"Hall's place will be rather exotic like that too that when it's finished in a year or so."

The taxi pulled up to a rather nondescript, but elegant, home set atop of a small ridge. Simon paid the driver and asked him to wait. The car idled behind them as they walked up the narrow stairs to the front door.

She'd read about Hall before and was struck with a nervous energy as Simon rapped on the door. He was supposedly quite an imposing and charismatic figure.

The door opened and a slim woman in a maid's uniform greeted them.

"Is Mr. Hall here?"

"Who is it?" a man's voice called from inside the house.

Elizabeth had seen pictures of Manly Hall before, but they didn't do him justice. He looked like a very handsome and very big Harry Houdini. With black hair and penetrating eyes, he cut an impressive figure. Considering the creepy creepiness of others of his ilk, Aleister Crowley and Max Heindel, Manly definitely got all the occult chicks.

"I'm Manly Hall," he said in a deep and yet gentle voice.

Simon introduced them and, without asking why they were there, Hall invited them in. Simon waved to dismiss the taxi and they joined Hall in his, well, hall.

"I'm a great admirer of your work," Simon said. "Your *Secret Teachings of All Ages* is seminal."

Hall was pleased. "You've read it?"

"Several times," Simon said. "I especially found your thoughts on alchemy and its exponents fascinating. In particular, the section on Paracelsus."

"Ah, yes."

"The depth of your research and understanding, it's astounding," Simon said. Elizabeth feared he was laying it on a little thick, but Hall seemed used to such effusive praise.

"Thank you," he said and then added, clasping his hands, "And how may I help you today?"

"I'm working on a paper myself. Nothing, of course, compared to your work, but I was wondering if you might allow access to some of your collection."

Hall looked them both over quickly and nodded. "Lovers of wisdom are always welcome."

Hall's library was immense, although obviously in a state of flux. Unsorted crates of books were stacked high along the far wall. "He seemed nice," Elizabeth said once Hall had left them alone to research.

"He's brilliant, but a classicist and more than a little anti-Semitic." Simon scanned the spines along the top shelf. "Ah, *Malleus Maleficarum* and *Grandier*." He pulled two large tomes off the shelf and handed Elizabeth one. "These will do to start."

For the next several hours they looked for something, anything that might give them a clue about how to help Alan. She read about Father Urbain Grandier, a French catholic priest who supposedly bewitched and bedded, with the help of several demons, a group of nuns in the early 1600's. The book even had plates depicting his contracts and signed by the demons themselves. Apparently, demons signed books like seventh grade girls, with little pictures and swooshes. She could swear one of them was actually a little heart. The priest had been promised "three days of whoring" for his soul. Not a good deal.

She read passages about the Osculum infame, or the Devil's kiss that supposedly sometimes sealed contracts with witches who'd promised allegiance to Satan. In one of them, the witch had to literally kiss the Devil's butt. Only men could come up with stuff like this. They did find a few more "contracts," but they were clearly little more than ancient religious propaganda.

From Popes to blues guitarists, people throughout the ages had claimed or been accused of pacts with the devil, but there was little actual evidence to support it. Simon and Elizabeth had even gone so far as to research a dozen or so of the so-called Devil's Bridges that were scattered throughout Europe. Each of them had a story, but none of them offered any help.

The entire day had come up seven and two and off-suit, until Simon found a small volume on Giuseppe Tartini, an eighteenth century Italian composer and violinist. Neither of them had ever seen the book before. Previous accounts of Tartini's life tangentially mentioned his deal with the devil. But this book went into great detail and the story it told was frighteningly familiar, right down to a drawing of the Devil's mark Tartini supposedly had on his forearm. It was a perfect match for the scar on Alan's arm. Worse yet, was the claim that Tartini had extended his contract several times over his lifetime by offering proxy souls—all of them women, and all of them apparently so deeply in love with him that they gave themselves willingly.

"Well, that's good, I guess, about the proxies," Elizabeth said, stretching her arms over her head to work out the kinks in her back.

"Is it?"

"I like Alan," Elizabeth said with a grin, "but my heart, and soul, belong to another."

Simon frowned and closed the book. "Let's hope that's enough."

Elizabeth leaned over and kissed him. "It always has been. I just wish we'd found something out that would help Alan."

"We're not beaten yet," Simon said with confidence, but she could tell he was worried, about her, about Alan, about all of it.

Truth be told, she was too.

THE BROWN DERBY WAS as fun and quirky on the inside as it was on the outside. The exterior was shaped like a giant derby hat, but actually extended into a long room in the interior. Two rows of plush, back-to-back, deep half-moon booths split the room down the middle. Tall dividers and the occasional strategically placed potted palm gave every table a feeling of intimacy and privacy. As she and Simon walked down the center aisle, Elizabeth could just imagine Lucy Ricardo looking over from her booth into William Holden's.

She spotted Jack sitting in a corner booth beneath a wall of the Derby's famous caricatures. He caught her eye and slipped out to greet them. Jack kissed her cheek and shook Simon's hand. "How'd the research go?"

"Mostly fruitless, I'm afraid," Simon said as he waited for Elizabeth to scooch into the center of the crescent-shaped booth before sliding in after her.

"There was fruit," Elizabeth said. "It wasn't much, but it did mirror Alan's experience."

Jack sat down opposite Simon. "That's good, right?"

"Well," Simon admitted, "it is something. However, I'm still far from convinced that what's happening with Thorn," he said lowering his voice, "is anything more than some sort of mesmerism or coercive persuasion."

Jack looked to Elizabeth for a translation.

"Mind control," she said.

"Really?" Jack sounded curious.

"Mesmer, Rasputin—" Simon said.

"Most of your Alan Rickman films," Elizabeth offered with a smile that was quickly quelled by Simon's unamused glare.

"Svengali," Simon finished. "There is ample evidence of people throughout history who had incredible powers of persuasion. Religious leaders, politicians. Even actors. Some cult leaders are able to use their personalities and the weakness of their followers to convince them to do unimaginable things, commit crimes and even suicide."

"I heard rumors about stuff like that during the war," Jack said. "Interrogation techniques, brainwashing, but…"

"And yet it happens." Simon unfolded his white linen napkin and placed it on his lap. "More often than we'd like to think."

"Have you ever wanted something so badly," Elizabeth asked Jack, "that you'd do anything for it?"

In a very un-Jacklike way, Jack toyed with the silverware of his place setting. He quickly noticed Elizabeth watching him, frowned and consciously tried to stop fidgeting.

Elizabeth filed his odd behavior away. "Imagine that someone incredibly charismatic comes along and tells you that he can give you what you want. For a price."

Jack shook his head. "Yeah, but saying you can do it and pulling it off are two different things."

"True, but—" Simon started to say, but fell silent as the waiter approached. They placed their orders and paused until the waiter left the table before continuing their conversation.

"Believing something is a powerful thing," Elizabeth said.

Jack sighed and Elizabeth saw his jaw work as if he were trying to keep from saying something. Finally, he settled on a distracted sounding, "Yeah."

Whatever was bothering Jack was big. Super-spy or not, they'd spent enough time together, unguarded honest time, for her to see that he was troubled.

Simon continued, oblivious to it. "The other complication is this notion of a proxy. That someone can be offered in a signee's stead."

"You mean trick somebody into taking their place?" Jack asked.

Elizabeth cast a quick glance at Simon and shook her head. "The other person has to do it willingly. Or at least that's what Alan and this book we found said."

"I'm taking both of those sources with a healthy dose of skepticism," Simon said. "I'm not sure we can trust Grant's judgment in this, and the book we found also claimed that listening to Tartini's sonata too frequently could result in insanity."

"Exhibit A: 'It's A Small World'."

"Elizabeth, this is hardly a joking matter," Simon said before turning his attention back to Jack. "My dear wife not only managed to get shot at yesterday, she also caught Thorn's eye. He told Grant that she would make an excellent trade should he chose to exercise that option in his contract."

Jack leaned forward, concern etched on his face. "I don't like the sound of that."

"No," Simon said. "Neither do I."

"Neither did Alan," Elizabeth said taking a sip from her water glass, "if anyone cares. Look, you shouldn't be worried about me—" Both men snorted and she chose to ignore that, "We should be worried about Alan. Whether we believe his deal is the real-deal or not, he does. And, in his mind, tomorrow, it expires and so does he."

Jack and Simon exchanged some testosterone-coded looks before Jack sat back in his seat. "What can I do to help?"

"I'm not sure," Simon said. "Did you learn anything else about Roth?"

Jack shrugged. "Not much more than what I told you on the phone. I haven't found any connection between him and the kid, but I'll keep digging." He scratched his chin in thought. "He's desperate enough to do something like that, though. We were at dinner last night at the Shooting Star, that's his favorite club, and I overheard a few people talking how bad business was and that the cops weren't biting on his deal. They can afford to wait him out though. They can get his properties for peanuts once his business dries up."

Abruptly, Jack ducked his head and Elizabeth turned to see what had alarmed him. "Speak of the devil," Jack said under his breath as he shifted in his seat, turning slightly into the booth.

"I thought that was you," Benny Roth said to Simon as he approached their table. "I didn't get a chance to thank you properly last night for saving my brother."

He stuck out his hand to Simon who reluctantly shook it. "We just happened to be in the right place at the right time."

"Modest," he said, looking more distrustful than impressed. "Most people'd be looking for a way to cash in."

Simon shook his head. "We're just glad everyone was safe."

"Good people are hard to find," Benny said, looking them both up and down in a way that made Elizabeth distinctly uncomfortable. He looked at Jack for the first time and frowned. "Do I know you?"

Jack looked up and smiled. "I don't think so."

Benny narrowed his eyes and looked a little harder. "You sure? I could swear—"

"I've just got one of those faces," Jack said as amiably and casually as possible.

"Yeah," Benny said, clearly not agreeing.

Whatever was going on, Jack obviously didn't want to be the center of Benny's attention.

"I was sorry to hear about Ruby," Elizabeth said, hoping to shift Benny's focus.

His eyes flashed to hers. They were like ice and then a cold smile lifted the corners of his mouth. It sent shivers up her spine and she had to consciously keep from flinching. Attention shifted, Elizabeth thought miserably.

"Did you know Ruby?" Benny asked.

"No, I was just—"

Simon reached across the table and squeezed Elizabeth's hand in a display of support, but what he really meant was: *Please, for the love of God, stop talking.*

"No," Simon said. "Sadly, we never had the chance. Your brother is all right, I take it?"

And the hot potato of Benny's attention changed hands again.

"Yeah," Benny said in a voice that wasn't exactly brimming over with brotherly love. "Thanks to you."

"Please give him our best," Simon said hoping to put an end to the conversation.

"I'll do that." Benny smirked and bowed his head in acknowledgement. "Enjoy your dessert."

He left the table and Elizabeth felt another shiver. She assuaged herself with the last bite of chocolate cake.

Simon glared at Elizabeth, clearly not pleased. "I don't know where to start. Drawing the ire of the local gangster or doing it by mentioning his dead girlfriend?"

"It was the first thing I could think of," Elizabeth said.

Jack raised a hand to stop Simon. "She was just trying to help. Maybe he did recognize me from one of the clubs," he added with a shrug, "I'd rather he didn't connect the dots, but there's not much of a picture if he does."

Simon grunted in displeasure, but had to agree with Jack. He gave Elizabeth one last frustrated look and then thoughtfully narrowed his eyes at Jack. "We?"

"We what?" Jack said.

Simon leaned forward and put his elbows on the table. "Before Roth came over you said 'we were at dinner'. Please tell me you were out with an informant and not out on a date with one of your conquests."

Jack looked down for a split second and then back up. "It's not like that."

Uh-oh. If it wasn't like *that* it was like something else, something worse. Worried and distracted Jack plus "we" and "it's not like that" equaled trouble. Elizabeth had never been very good at math, but she could put two and two together.

Simon was apparently way ahead of her. He shook his head and raised his eyebrows. "A woman? How many times did we go over the risks involved in your being here?"

Jack raised his hands in submission. "Don't worry. I get it."

"Do you?" Simon said. "A seemingly insignificant change to your life here can have serious repercussions in the future."

Despite the fact that Jack offered a quick, "I know," Elizabeth knew him well enough to see that he was still working through it all. And for a woman to unbalance someone like Jack, whatever was going on had to be big or bad, or love.

Relationships were his kryptonite. At first, Elizabeth had thought it was just the life of a spy—never letting himself get too close to anyone. But, Jack had dropped a few hints in conversations, when he was alone with her, when his guard was down. Somewhere along the way, he'd fallen in love and been burned. So badly, that he'd never really let anyone get close again. If he was serious about this woman, it was serious.

"This woman," Simon said. "Is she someone your other self knows? Is involved with?"

"It's under control," Jack said tightly.

"Is it?" Simon said. "If you do something here that alters your own past—a past that Elizabeth and I are part of—is it still under control? Is any...liaison," Simon said lingering over the word significantly, "worth that?"

Simon didn't see it, but Elizabeth did. Just the slightest wince at the word. This was definitely more than one of Jack's usual casual encounters. There was nothing casual about the pain in his eyes. Elizabeth's heart filled and broke for him in the same instant. Congratulations on your doomed romance.

Oblivious to Jack's pain, Simon leaned forward and his hands clenching into fists as he tried to keep a check on his own growing worry. "If you are doing something that changes the original 1933 Jack's life, something that led him to not enlist or join another branch of the service, have you seriously considered the consequences?"

Jack looked away again, sighed and nodded. His shoulders fell a little as he sat back in his seat. "You already gave me this lecture." His protest was half-hearted and she could see he was silently castigating himself.

"And I'm going to give it to you again," Simon said. "Because here's what happens. You aren't in the OSS, so you aren't assigned to London. No one is there to stop King Zog's men from shooting Elizabeth. If by miracle she survives that and isn't imprisoned, without your help she's...tortured by

Nazis, we're both probably killed. But that's hardly worst of it. Without your help, the Shard is surely lost. The Nazis gain control of it. Power shifts and the allies lose the war."

Wow. Simon Cross, painter of bleak pictures, now available for children's parties and bar mitzvahs. Elizabeth chewed her bottom lip in worry. Between Simon's dire predictions and Jack's demeanor, she felt a little queasy.

"So, as you can see," Simon said, leaning back, "I do worry. And with good reason."

"You don't know that's how it'll be," Jack said.

"Is that a risk you're really willing to take?" Simon said.

Jack stared down at his empty plate and when he looked up, it was the most serious she'd ever seen him. He looked at Elizabeth briefly with a mixture of apology and reassurance. And then turned to Simon. There was no trace of his usual lighthearted charm and he met Simon's gaze with a steel glare and a hint of melancholy. He didn't say anything, but the answer was in his eyes. A man like Jack, who'd given everything for his country, who'd risked his life over and over for the cause, had one more sacrifice to make.

Chapter Fifteen

THE MIDDAY SUN REFLECTED off the concrete of the studio. Being between the ground and buildings, it was like standing in a kiln. Elizabeth fanned herself with the script to *Through the Dark Continent,* which was at least good for something, and wondered at the mystery that was her husband.

Simon looked at the bicycle with far less distaste than she'd expected. In fact, he seemed almost amused. He shrugged off his jacket and folded it into the basket that hung off the handlebars.

"It's a long walk," Mr. Fox said seeing Elizabeth's expression of mistrust.

She nodded and he waved as he headed back into the writers' building.

She and Simon had come to the studio to talk to Alan. It still amazed her that he'd come to work today. All morning she'd felt the clock ticking down toward midnight. If his contract was real, it was scheduled to expire tonight. If she had less than a day to live, she wouldn't spend it here. Or maybe it was Alan's way of pretending none of it was happening.

Whatever his reasons, he'd come to work and if they were going to find him, they had to get to Lot Three, which was apparently too far to walk. Sadly, golf carts had not made it to the big time yet. Limited private cars were allowed to drive through the studio and Simon and Elizabeth, as low-level writers, didn't rate. The studio's trolley route wouldn't get them much nearer than they already were. That left one option—bicycles. They were the main source of transportation around the lot and in high demand. Luckily, Mr. Fox and Mr. Owl had offered theirs.

The bikes were big, clunky beach cruiser types with broad handlebars and fat tires. "You do know how to ride, don't you?" she said with a grunt as she hefted the heavy bike out of its slot in the rack.

Simon pulled his bike out of the rack without nearly the same effort. "We do have bicycles in England, Elizabeth."

"I know, but it's just hard to picture you on one."

He got onto the bike and held out his arms. "Behold."

He actually looked quite at home, despite the incongruity of wearing a suit.

Elizabeth's bike was a little too big for her, and worst of all, a man's bike, but there wasn't a choice. She glared at the bike's crossbar and tried to figure out what to do with her skirt. Finally, she hiked it up just enough to fling her leg over the seat and straddle the crossbar, on tiptoes.

Simon snickered.

"You try it in a skirt," she said. She'd ridden bikes all her life, but never one like this and never in a dress.

Simon smiled and easily pushed off. He rode around in lazy circles while she continued to fumble. Her legs were too short, the seat was too high and the dress was getting in the way.

"You can always ride," he offered as he circled past her, "on my handlebars," he finished with another pass.

"I can do it." And she did, just barely. She planted her right foot on the pedal, which she couldn't see because of the flare in her skirt, pushed down and prayed. The bike wobbled beneath her until her left foot found its place and she gave it another pedal. Another pedal and she was fine. Once the bike had forward momentum, it stabilized and she sat down.

She started down Main Street trying to remember the directions Mr. Fox had given them. She could make it as long as she didn't have to stop. Ever.

Once they left the main studio lot, which was filled with sound stages, production buildings and offices, they hit the backlot. Or at least one of them. Mammoth Studios was well named. The backlots covered dozens and dozens of acres and were a crazy mishmash of times and places.

They rode past a Spanish hacienda where, on the steps, men in dashing red and white uniforms fought with swords while bloodied comrades had lunch at a nearby craft services table. There was a replica of somewhere on the left bank in Paris where a couple ran up a cobblestone street under a downpour of rain from a giant sprinkler system above them. A quaint square straight out of small town anywhere USA was empty except for a few people staring up at the clock tower making notes.

All of the buildings looked genuine enough from the front if you didn't look too closely. It was only as you passed that you saw the beams and struts holding up the façades. It was all sort of dreamlike—snatches of disparate things, images that never really took hold, a living montage.

They were stopped for filming at one crossroad and Elizabeth barely managed not to tip over. To their right was a long frontage for a New York Street and to the left a long narrow river with sets dressed to look like somewhere in the Netherlands. They passed a Chinese street, a cemetery and two more New York streets before making it to the outskirts of Lot Three and the enormous sets for Alan's ill-fated last film, *Through the Dark Continent*.

There were two main sets and several smaller set-ups each designed to look like deepest darkest Africa, or at least Hollywood's version of it. The main village set had several thatched huts in front of a jungle backdrop that consisted of a few native California trees like Eucalyptus with fake vines hung over the branches, large exposed jungle tree roots and lots and lots of large potted banana and palm trees. A few of the "natives" sat around a card table playing poker as they waited for their next scene.

Most of the focus was on the other major set piece—a forty-foot tall temple, made out of rough-hewn rock carved out of a cliff-face. Elizabeth shaded her eyes against the bright sun as she looked at the set. At various levels of the temple small clusters of natives dressed in leather thongs, feathers, and body paint pounded the staffs of their spears into the rock as they stomped in rhythm and chanted something unintelligible. Two big cats, a lion and a tiger paced the inside of their cages, embedded in the cliff.

Simon whispered in her ear and pointed toward a small group of intrepid adventurers as they made their way up a twisty path that led to the top level of the temple. Alan was at the head of the group of explorers and just about to greet a skinny old tribal chieftain with a ridiculously enormous headdress.

If there were thirty people on the set there were easily twice as many behind the cameras. Some held cables and other equipment, while others stood by lights and reflective panels. A half dozen men stood on a ten-foot wooden platform with a camera mounted at the top and at least a dozen more centered around a large camera crane that rose up nearly thirty feet in the air.

"Come on, natives, you can give me more than that!" a man with a bullhorn yelled. "Chant harder for God's sake!"

The natives did.

"Keep going, Alan, good! You're nearly there!" the man yelled again. "Get ready, Morty!"

Alan, dressed as the great explorer Stanley, reached the top level of the temple. He took off his pith helmet and bowed.

"Now, Morty!"

The little old chieftain raised his hands to the sky and joined in the chant. Alan staggered back a step as a five-foot long ape hand rose up from behind the mountain. The chanting got faster, louder. The chief turned to greet the giant beast and his headdress fell off.

"Cut!"

Instantly, the chanting stopped. The little old man shrugged and tried to put the headdress back on. Another man popped out from behind the giant ape hand to see what was going on.

"Damn it. Wardrobe!"

Alan laughed and clapped the old man on the back. Then, he turned and shielded his eyes against the glare of the sun as he waited for direction.

Someone whispered in the director's ear. He held up his megaphone. "That's lunch!" He stormed off with a retinue of people apologizing in his wake.

Several men scrambled up the rock and helped the natives and adventurers navigate the dangerous climb back down. Once he was on terra firma again, Elizabeth called out to Alan.

He waved back and met them just in front of the main camera rig. "Well, hello," he said with a broad smile. There was no hint of the morose man they'd left the other night or the one she'd spoken to on the phone yesterday. "What do you think?" he said waving at the emptying set.

"Amazing," Elizabeth said, feeling a tingle of excitement. It was all so absurd and wonderful.

Simon on the other hand…

Alan noticed his frown. "Something wrong?"

"Well," Simon said. "Tigers are not indigenous to the African continent."

Alan put a hand on his shoulder. "Neither are fifty foot apes, my dear fellow." He turned him toward the long line of picnic tables. "Now, how about lunch?"

A long buffet had been set up under tents adjacent to the set. With the precision of a Roman legion the caterers fed over one hundred members of the cast and crew. Elizabeth, Simon and Alan joined the other members of his "expedition" at a table in the shade of a large oak across the dirt street from the set. Alan regaled the group with stories of his early pictures.

After lunch was over, she and Simon took him aside. For a man with hours to live, Alan seemed undisturbed, even happy. He was acting like it was just a normal day. Elizabeth was filled with a mixture of awe and concern. If she thought she had one day to live, she's pretty sure she wouldn't spend it at work as though nothing were wrong. But, then again, UCSB was a far cry from Mammoth Studios.

"What should I do?" Alan said as he leaned against a tree and lit a cigarette. "This," he said through an exhale, "is who I am."

"You could leave here," Elizabeth said. She hated to run from anything, but sometimes getting the heck out of Dodge was the best choice. "Maybe if you can get away from him…"

"My dear," he said with a sad smile. "An actor never leaves Hollywood behind. Hollywood leaves him."

"All right, let's try it again!" the director yelled through his bullhorn.

"Try not to worry," he said, gently touching her cheek. "I've had a good run."

Elizabeth's heart sank at his words.

"That damn head-thing better stay on this time!" the director cried. "Alan!"

Alan crushed out his cigarette and started for the set. "Come by the house at six!" he called over his shoulder before turning around. "And put on your best. We're going out tonight!"

And just like that he joined the rest of the cast as they took their places for another take.

Simon's arm wrapped around her waist. "There's nothing more we can do, Elizabeth." His voice was comforting, but resigned.

Why was everyone so ready to just give up? She looked back up at Alan climbing to the top of the set. Stanley didn't give up and she wasn't going to either. "There's one thing we haven't tried."

"What's that?"

"Thorn."

SIMON WISHED, AND NOT for the first time, that he could throw Elizabeth over his shoulder and carry her away to somewhere safe. Of course, he couldn't and, the longer he spent with her, the more he realized that when it came to Elizabeth, nowhere would be safe enough. Certainly though, going to see Thorn was just about as far from safe as he could imagine.

When Thorn's secretary told them that he wasn't in today, Simon felt the relief of a last reprieve. That was until Elizabeth asked for and was given Thorn's home address.

If Thorn hadn't shown an interest in Elizabeth, Simon might have almost willingly gone along with her foolish plan. Under the current circumstances, it was unthinkable. There was a difference, he pointed out, in seeing a lion in a cage at the zoo and walking out into the jungle and sticking your damn head in its mouth. It was madness. At that, he drew the line, and Elizabeth promptly stepped over it.

She gave his hand a reassuring squeeze as they walked up the front steps to Thorn's Beverly Hills home. Simon looked down at her in wonder. Perhaps she was the one with mind control powers.

Of course, she'd been right. They'd come all this way, risked everything so far; they had to at least try to confront Thorn. It was, he hated to admit, the right thing to do. Not just right in the sense of helping Grant, but in the grander scheme. She'd seen their place in that plan long before he had. It was, no doubt, her openness to the world that let her see it. And, it was, he felt with no joy in the irony, her openness that worried him the most.

He'd always been a man who lived behind walls, first at Grey Hall and then of his own creation. She'd managed to find a way inside them. However, as much as she'd like to think she had, she hadn't torn them down. He'd merely rebuilt them with her inside. Of course, that didn't last, couldn't last. Elizabeth saw to that.

"Ready?" she asked as she reached for the doorbell.

He wasn't; they weren't, but it wasn't for lack of trying. When he'd finally reluctantly agreed to see Thorn, he'd done so on the condition that she learn mental techniques to try to keep Thorn at bay.

Elizabeth had said something about Occlumency and some Professor Snape. He'd merely nodded, not having any idea what she meant, and instructed her on the few methods he'd come across in his studies. Primarily, they were ways of focusing the mind on positive things—an anchor for thought and emotion. None of them were designed for whatever it was Thorn might be doing, but it was the only defense they had. Assuming, of course, as Elizabeth pointed out, he wasn't an agent of the dark lord. Then, all bets were off.

Simon heard footsteps approaching from behind the door and held on to Elizabeth's hand a little more tightly. A butler in full dress opened the door and invited them to wait in the front parlor.

Thorn's home was elegant and tasteful. Simon wasn't sure what he'd expected. Heads mounted on the wall? A necklace of ears? In an odd way, that might have been more comforting than the beautiful, far too normal home they'd stepped into. It would have been preferable to see Thorn for the monster he was. This veil of charm was more dangerous than fangs.

After a few moments, the butler returned. "Mr. Thorn is waiting for you in his office."

"Remember your focus point," Simon said, tapping his chest, as they were led through the foyer. "Everything will be all right."

She smiled up at him. "I know."

Thorn sat behind a large mahogany desk. He lifted his head and smiled in a way that made Simon rethink his abandoned, throw-Elizabeth-over-his-shoulder strategy.

"Come in," Thorn said. "I've been wondering when you might stop by."

He rose from his chair and came around the desk to greet them. Simon and Elizabeth didn't walk too far into the room. They stayed on the far edge of the Persian rug, sure to keep some distance between Thorn and them.

Thorn gestured to the chairs in front of his desk. "Please?"

"No, thank you," Simon said. They wanted to stay alert and focused.

Thorn shrugged diffidently and leaned back against the front of his desk. "As you wish. Although," he said turning his attention to Elizabeth, "you can't really appreciate my collection from there."

He drew their attention to a large case mounted on the wall behind his desk. Behind the glass, pinned to black velvet were dozens of butterflies, their iridescent wings open as if caught in midflight.

"Aren't they beautiful?" he said, almost lovingly. "These are a few of my favorites."

Simon looked down at Elizabeth and saw the anger and disgust in her eyes. He squeezed her hand. "We're here to discuss Alan Grant."

Thorn didn't look away from his collection. "Are you?"

"Yes," Elizabeth said. "We want you to release him from his…contract."

Thorn chuckled. "Do you?" He eased off the desk, walked back around it and sat down again. "Surely, that's a matter between Grant and the studio."

"That isn't what she meant," Simon said.

Thorn placed his palms on the edge of the blotter on his desk and pushed himself back more deeply into his chair. "No?"

Elizabeth started forward, but Simon's touch on her arm kept her where she was. "You know what we're talking about."

"I'm sure I don't," Thorn said. "Why don't you tell me?"

"Your agreement with Grant," Simon said sharply. "Whatever coercion you used, it won't work in the end."

"Coercion? Is that what he told you?" Thorn steepled his fingers in front of him and looked at Simon in a way that felt as though the man was seeing right through his soul. Simon's hand slid down Elizabeth's arm and gripped her hand tightly. Focus.

Thorn touched his index fingers to his lips. "No, I don't think he did. He told you the truth."

Simon tamped down his growing feelings of unease. "What he thinks is the truth."

"And you're unconvinced." Thorn leaned forward. "It might be fun to convince you," he said more to himself than to them.

"Whoever," Simon said, struggling to keep his mind clear, "whatever you think you are, it doesn't matter to me."

"Oh, but it does," Thorn said with a soft laugh. "So much, so *very* much." His eyes shifted to Elizabeth.

Simon's heart stuttered and then raced. He could feel his control slipping away. He gripped Elizabeth's hand even more tightly and clenched his other hand into a fist. This man standing in front of him was flesh and blood, he told himself. This was no devil he was talking to. Just a man. "Your lies won't work on us."

"The only lies I need are the ones you tell yourself," Thorn said. "You're quite adept at that aren't you, Cross?"

The tension in Simon's muscles intensified until he could hear the rapid thrumming of his own heart.

"I can give you what you want," Thorn said, and then he glanced at Elizabeth. "I can keep her safe."

The sound of his own blood rushing through his ears was white noise against the world.

Simon.

The voice sounded like it was underwater—distant and muffled, but insistent. "Simon…Simon!"

He felt her tug on his arm and, still dazed, he turned to look at her. Elizabeth's eyes were wide with worry. "Focus," she said, cupping his cheeks and forcing him to look into her eyes. "Remember? Focus on me."

Simon felt the clouds begin to part, and Elizabeth turned to Thorn. She pulled herself to her full five foot four and met Thorn's gaze with a calm assurance Simon envied. "Our souls are not for sale."

Despite the confidence in her declaration, Thorn didn't seemed convinced, but didn't press the matter. "We'll see."

Elizabeth didn't relent. "We're here about Alan Grant."

Thorn grew instantly bored and waved a dismissive hand in the air. "There's no point in that. His contract has nearly been fulfilled."

Simon pushed the last bit of haze from his mind. "We'd like to see it. The contract."

"I'm afraid only the contract holder has the right to ask that."

"That's convenient," Simon said. "A contract no one else can see."

"I assure you, they are quite legitimate. I went to great lengths to ensure my contract was drawn up according to the laws of man. Jurisdictional issues and all." Thorn smiled. "In my line of work, you become well acquainted with quite a few attorneys."

"What do you get out of it?" Elizabeth asked suddenly.

Thorn shrugged. "Their souls."

"Assuming that's possible," Elizabeth continued. "Why?"

Thorn was surprised at that. He arched an eyebrow and put down the pen he'd been toying with. "In all my years, which are considerable, no one has ever thought to ask me that. Fascinating." He paused to give the matter some thought. "I'm not sure I can put this in a way you can understand."

"Try me," Elizabeth said lifting her chin defiantly.

Thorn's eyes lit up; he obviously enjoyed the sparring. Simon did not.

"I began because I enjoyed the challenge and the pride in collecting something valuable. A man has nothing of greater value than his soul. But now...I think it's what I'm meant to do. It's who I am. It's why I'm here. Do you understand?"

"Yes," she said. "We feel the same way."

"Do you?"

"We're here to stop you," she said. "That's who we are."

Thorn smiled, amused. "Pity," he said as he leaned back in his chair. "Time is not on your side."

"We still have a day left."

Thorn grinned. "Less than that."

Elizabeth narrowed her eyes and smiled as if she had the most wonderful secret in the world. "You're not the only one with a few tricks up his sleeve."

Thorn arched an eyebrow in expectant pleasure. "I look forward to it."

What in God's name was she talking about? Simon gripped Elizabeth's arm and edged her toward the door.

"Me too," she said as if they were arguing about next week's football match.

When Simon had finally led her out of the room and out of Thorn's home, he turned to her and asked, "What was that all about?"

"I don't know," she said angrily. "He makes me cranky."

Simon ignored that and led her further down the street. The farther away from Thorn they got, the better. "And the tricks we have up our sleeves?"

"It's a bluff."

Simon sighed, although he knew that was going to be her answer.

Elizabeth surprised him and stopped walking. "Daddy always said, when you get a handful of nothing, bet 'em like you got 'em."

She looked up at him with such fierce resolve he almost believed her.

"Yes, but wasn't your father a rather poor poker player?" Simon said as kindly as he could.

Elizabeth's face crumpled. "I was hoping you wouldn't remember that."

Jack leaned back against the warm sand and felt it cling to his wet skin. The sun hung low in the sky and cast a bright yellow path from West to East along the surface of the ocean. Betty walked back and forth along the shore as the gentle breakers foamed around her ankles. She looked up and waved at him. He lifted a sandy arm and waved back. It was the beginning of their goodbye.

He knew after dinner with Simon and Elizabeth that it had to end. Hell, he knew before then. Even before Cross' warnings, he'd sensed deep down inside that this couldn't be. He'd thought losing her the first time had been hard, but it was nothing compared to this. Every moment was a torture.

She walked toward him, her hips swaying as her feet dug into the softening sand.

"That was great," she said, bending down to pick up a towel and drying off. "We sure don't have that in Fort Wayne."

When she'd asked him to come here today, he should have said no. He should have broken it off right then and there. But he hadn't. He wanted one last day, one last day to sear everything into his memory including the pain. He deserved that and more.

Betty wrapped the towel around her as if she'd just come from the shower and sat down next to him. The setting sun made her skin look like gold. She leaned in to Jack and bumped him with her elbow. "You in there?"

She smiled at him and the wind blew a wet tendril of hair across her eyes. She brushed it away and tilted her head. "John?"

"I'm fine," he lied. How many had he told? "Just," he said, nodding toward the ocean, "it makes you think."

She leaned into his side and wrapped an arm across his back. He felt her soft cheek rest on his shoulder as she gazed out at the ocean. It was wonderful and perfect and he'd never been so miserable.

He'd been a damn fool to have started it in the first place. Deep down, he must have known it would end this way. Could only end this way.

God, he'd been so selfish. He'd wanted her and everything else had fallen away. He'd put all the people he cared for at risk, the whole damn war at risk, just to be near her. And he was being punished for it now. If he'd just stayed in the shadows that day in the alley or walked away any of the days since, this wouldn't hurt so damn much. And, of course, he thought with a sinking feeling in the pit of his stomach, in the end, he'd ended up hurting her the most. Or he would, when he finally found the courage to say goodbye.

Just one more sacrifice for the war.

He felt Betty shiver and burrow closer to him for warmth. "What do you think for dinner tonight? Maybe that little Italian place again?"

"I can't," he said and she leaned away. Jack sat up and pulled one knee toward his chest. "My sister and husband have some event or something, and I'm supposed to go and be supportive."

Betty was disappointed, but she tossed her head to the side. "That just means more meatballs for me."

"I'm sorry," he said, wishing she could know how much and knowing she never would.

Every scenario—his staying, her leaving and none of them could be. This could never be.

"That's okay," she said waving it off. "We can go tomorrow."

"Sure," he said. He brushed some sand from her shoulder. "I'll miss you."

"It's just one night, silly." She leaned in and kissed him. Just a quick, reassuring kiss, but he caught her cheek in his hand as she started to pull away. He looked into her eyes and then down to her lips and gently guided her mouth back to his. Her lips were soft and tender.

When the kiss was over, she eased back and looked at him in such an odd way. Whatever it was in her eyes, it passed. She smiled and turned back to watch the sun kiss the horizon. He watched her and felt his heart ache and knew that it would never go away.

Chapter Sixteen

Simon and Elizabeth went over everything they'd seen, everything they'd learned again, looking for some clue, any clue to help them save Alan. There must have been something they'd overlooked. Elizabeth refused to accept anything else.

They'd called Alan to see if they could look at his copy of the contract, but of course, he didn't have one. "Paperwork was never my strong suit," he'd said.

She and Simon talked in circles through the rest of the afternoon until a knock on the door interrupted them. A messenger carried in several large boxes, a bouquet of flowers and a note from Alan. They were cordially invited to his house for cocktails, formal attire required. God only knew what Alan was planning for his last night. Or what he saw as his last night, Elizabeth corrected herself. Even if he saw it that way, she wasn't ready to give up. For now, though, all they could do was stay with Alan and be there when the time came and hope for a solution.

Elizabeth reread Alan's note, looking for some clue as to what he had planned for tonight, but all it said was something about "cocktails and fun". Formal fun.

Simon still had his tuxedo, but Elizabeth's only formal dress was still in need of repair. Of course, Alan knew that and had taken the liberty of sending several gowns for her to choose from. A small token of thanks, the note had said, for their friendship.

Every dress fit perfectly, not too surprising considering Alan was hardly a novice when it came to women's figures. Elizabeth settled on the pale gold silk brocade floor length gown. The red was too wicked city woman and the black, well, she refused to think about how that one made her feel. Alan had also sent a white fur stole. Elizabeth wasn't comfortable with the idea of wearing fur, but it was a cool evening, by Los Angeles standards, and she couldn't bring herself to do anything to insult Alan's generosity.

At six o'clock the front desk rang letting them know that a car had arrived for them. Alan had certainly thought of everything.

The drive to his home was quiet. Simon tried to reassure her that the night wasn't over. They would stay with him through the night and when midnight came, they'd find a way. She just wished Alan didn't seem so resigned to it all. He obviously loved being a movie star, but if he just had something else to live for? Or someone, she thought as the car turned up Camden Drive. Walking down the side of the road was a familiar figure. It was the girl who'd been at Alan's the other day. Elizabeth had a hunch and called for the driver to pull over.

"What on earth are you doing?" Simon asked as she jumped out of the car.

She poked her head back in through the open door. "Following a hunch. You go ahead and I'll catch up."

"Elizabeth—"

She pointed at Grant's driveway barely one hundred feet up the road. "It's right there. I want to talk to the girl. Alone."

Simon swallowed his protest and nodded curtly. Elizabeth closed the door and the car pulled away.

Elizabeth hurried to catch up. "Wait!" The girl either didn't hear her or didn't want to talk and continued down the street. Elizabeth lifted the hem of her dress and dashed across the street. "Girl from Alan Grant's!"

Finally, she stopped and turned. Elizabeth waved to her and caught up.

She looked at Elizabeth with a worried expression, taking in the dress and the fur. "Are you his girlfriend?"

"Alan's? No. Just a friend. A good friend."

The girl glanced nervously up the street and frowned. "Who's he?"

Elizabeth followed her gaze. Simon stood at the end of the driveway, watching and waiting, and trying to be discreet. "He's my husband." She waved him away. "Ignore him. I'm more interested in who you are."

The girl's forehead creased and she nervously tucked a blonde curl behind her ear. When she looked back up at Elizabeth with her pale blue eyes, Elizabeth knew she couldn't be anyone else. "You're his daughter, aren't you?"

Her wobbly chin was all the reply Elizabeth needed. "Grace," she said and fresh tears started to spill.

Elizabeth slipped an arm over Grace's slender shoulders as they trembled. "It's all right, honey. Let's go on up to the house."

Elizabeth eased her around, but she shook her head. "They'll just send me away again."

Elizabeth narrowed her eyes. "Not this time." She hugged her to her side. "Trust me?"

Grace looked a little dubious, but she nodded.

"Good."

Elizabeth led her up the street to where Simon waited for them. He arched an eyebrow and offered a tentative, "Hello."

Grace gave him a weak smile.

"Would you keep *her father* occupied," Elizabeth said with a not so subtle nod toward Grace. "While we have a little chat?"

Simon's eyes widened in surprise. "Of course," he said and gave Elizabeth his patented *what are you doing now?* expression. She returned it with a glare and he knew enough not to press the point.

Grace sniffled loudly. Simon's attention shifted to the girl. He frowned and then reached into his tuxedo jacket, pulling out a handkerchief. He held it out to the girl. She looked at it uneasily until his expression softened. "It will be all right," he said gently.

She smiled gratefully and took the handkerchief. Elizabeth gave Simon's hand a quick thank you squeeze which earned her a *don't make me regret* it look.

The three of them silently walked up the drive. When they reached the front door, Peter was standing there looking very uncomfortable.

"I'll take responsibility," Elizabeth assured him.

Peter looked anxiously from the girl to Elizabeth and then to Simon.

"Is there a place where the two of us can talk?" Elizabeth asked.

Peter frowned, but nodded and escorted them to the study. Grace looked around the room anxiously and wouldn't sit until Elizabeth told her it was all right. Elizabeth brought her a glass of water from a carafe by the desk. She took a tiny sip. Poor kid, Elizabeth thought, as she took off her ridiculous fur stole and sat down on the ottoman. She looked closely at the girl. Her clothes were simple and conservative and her tears were certainly genuine.

"How long have you been trying to see him?"

"About a week," Grace said, putting the glass of water on the end table. "I came all the way from Philadelphia."

"That's a long way."

The girl nodded proudly. "I saved up. Momma didn't want me to come, but said I had a right to meet him."

"You've never met?"

Grace shook her head. "I just found out who he was."

Elizabeth heard Simon's voice in her head. A gold digger? The mother looking for money and sending the child? People probably tried to put the touch on men like Alan Grant all the time.

Grace seemed to sense Elizabeth's train of thought and said quickly, "I'm not here for money or anything like that. I just…I lived my whole life not knowing my father and then I find out who he is. And, I know it's silly, but I felt like I kind of did know him. From his movies."

Elizabeth nodded. "It's not silly."

"And then I had enough saved and I wanted to see for myself if the man I saw up there is who he really was." Her cheeks trembled. "But he won't even see me. I just want him to see me."

Elizabeth covered Grace's hand with hers. "And he will."

Ten minutes later when Elizabeth finally joined Simon and Alan in his living room, she wasn't sure whether to just cry or cry and then hit someone. The poor girl endured nights with relatives who thought she was foolish for trying and days waiting for her father to let her in the front door. That ended tonight.

"So glad you could join us," Alan said as he held up a drink for her and gestured to Simon. "Your husband's been about as much fun as an empty bottle of gin. Barely said two words. We still have a few hours before the premier though..." Her expression swiftly wiped the smile off his face. "What's the matter?"

"That's what I was going to ask you," Elizabeth said. "I just had a very interesting conversation with a very distraught young girl."

Alan started to put the drink he'd offered her down and decided to drink it himself instead. "I appreciate your concern—"

"My concern?" Elizabeth was not going to be put off. "That girl is your daughter."

No matter how practiced an actor Alan was he couldn't hide the shame and the pain he felt in that moment. Elizabeth tried to make sense of it, to come to Alan's defense in her head, but she simply couldn't.

"There is nothing you can say to me that I haven't already said to myself," Alan said.

"You're an ass," Simon said.

"Including that." Alan put his empty glass down and stared into the crystal for a moment. "It's far better this way, don't you think? Considering my rather imminent demise."

"No, I don't think." Elizabeth tried to control her anger. "All she wants to do is see you. To see her father. Doesn't she deserve that at least? Don't you love her at all?"

"Of course I do!" Alan said and then again more softly. "Of course I do."

Simon shook his head, glowering at Alan. "What sort of man abandons his own child?"

"She was better off without me," he said quickly. "They both were."

Alan picked up and put down his empty glass.

"I don't believe that," Elizabeth said.

"I am not a hero," Alan said softly. "I am not that man you see up on the screen. I am flesh and blood and flawed." Alan's blue eyes filled with deep pain and regret. "Feet of clay, my dear, feet of clay," he said before walking a few slow paces to a chair and sinking into it. "I want to see her very, very much, but now…" He shook his head. "She deserves far more than I can give her."

"You're her father."

"I am a dead man," he said.

Elizabeth looked at this man she'd so admired and saw the truth. "You're afraid."

"Yes," he said in a voice barely more than a whisper. "I am a coward. I ran away from her and her mother years ago and I haven't stopped yet."

"It isn't too late," Elizabeth said. "She's amazing."

Pride flashed across Alan's face before he shoved it away. "All the more reason to send her away. If Thorn should see her…" He shook his head, dispelling the thought.

"Go see her," Elizabeth said. "Just spend a little time with her and we'll keep her away from Thorn, I promise. Give her an hour. You owe her that at the very least."

Elizabeth could see his resolve weakening. "My father died when I was seventeen. And I would give anything to see him again, even if it was just for an hour."

She held out her hand to Alan. "She's waiting."

Alan took her hand and stood. He reached out and gently touched her cheek. "Oh, Lucia."

Alan's eyes were wet as he nodded and took a deep, bracing breath. He walked to the door and paused. He didn't turn back, but asked, "You'll wait?"

"We'll be here."

ALAN SPENT THE NEXT hour talking with his daughter. What they said, Elizabeth didn't ask, but when they saw him again, Alan looked like a man who'd just learned Santa Claus was real—stunned and delighted and unsure of his strange new reality. He seemed ready to face anything, even Thorn. Maybe he finally had something real to live for.

Peter dropped off Grace at her aunt's house and came back to take Alan to the premiere. Elizabeth was a little surprised he still wanted to go, but as he put it, tonight could be his final performance as Alan Grant and he was going to enjoy it.

As their limousine pulled onto Hollywood Boulevard, Elizabeth could see the giant searchlights scanning the night sky in the distance. Huge ten-foot cutouts of showgirl's legs caught in mid-kick were strung up along the street lamps like Christmas decorations. The sidewalks were packed with people trying to get a glimpse of their favorite star.

They drove past the theater and Elizabeth strained to see out of the back window. Grauman's Chinese Theatre was magnificent. The front part of the façade rose nearly one hundred feet in the air and was flanked by two gigantic coral red columns that were capped by wrought iron masks and a bronze roof. Between the columns an enormous dragon carved from stone and two giant Foo Dogs guarded the entrance. Standing over the main entrance was a thirty-foot pair of showgirl legs and the signature sign of the movie premiering, "Chorus Girl!"

Their limousine u-turned in front of a police barricade and lined up with the other cars pulling up in front of the red carpet. Fans clamored to see inside the car. When it was their turn, Alan smiled happily and said, "Once more unto the breach, dear friends. And try to have some fun," he added with a grin.

As Elizabeth stepped out of the car, the flashbulbs and cries to "look here" were overwhelming. Alan stood on one side and Simon on the other as they paused to give the press a few good shots. In front of them, an actual red carpet showed the path toward the forecourt of the theater. A voice boomed over loudspeakers that Alan Grant and friends had arrived and a cheer went up as the crowd pressed against the velvet ropes and security guards.

Alan soaked it all in—the screaming, noise, the people reaching out to touch him. His eyes glittered in the bright lights.

"A marvelous chaos, isn't it?" Alan said, before urging her to walk with him up the carpet.

The three of them paused in the middle of the path for another set of pictures. Simon shifted uncomfortably next to her and frowned at the crowd, looking more like a bodyguard than a dashing escort. But he was dashing and so was Alan and the frenzy of energy was making her skin tingle. Not to mention that she was standing in the famous forecourt of Grauman's Chinese Theatre where stars had left their legacies in the shape of hand and footprints in cement.

She idly wondered who she was standing on when another gentle tug on her elbow signaled it was time to move again. That's when she saw the large, heavy-set man straining the confines of his tuxedo vest. He smiled broadly and leaned into the two tall microphones standing in front of him. She didn't recognize the call letters emblazoned on the halos, but it was clear this was a big media event being broadcast live on the radio. "Alan Grant, ladies and gentlemen! Perhaps we can get him to stop in and say a word."

Alan's grin broadened as he stepped to the microphones and shook the man's hand. "Hello, Tom."

The man smiled and stepped back. Alan looked out over the crowd. "They say movies are magic. And I quite agree. But the real magic isn't the talent of the wonderful people who brought you tonight's picture or any other. It's you."

The buzz of the crowd died down, perhaps sensing something special about this moment.

Alan looked out over the crowd, as in love with them as they were with him. He pointed out toward the throng, slowly moving his arm to encompass all of them. "When you walk through those doors," he said pointing to the entrance to the theater, "you bring the magic with you. You open your hearts and minds to the impossible and believe. *That's* the magic of the movies. You. And I humbly thank you for letting me be a small part of it. Thank you. Good night."

Alan waved once more to the crowd and stepped back. The crowd applauded politely, unsure what to make of anything so heartfelt. Elizabeth and Simon moved to join Alan when the announcer jumped in their way. "And look who we have here! Mr. and Mrs. Cross, the heroes who joined Alan Grant in saving Sam Roth's life. Won't you say a few words?"

Elizabeth looked to Alan for help, but he merely chuckled and nodded toward the microphone, mouthing the words "have fun."

Elizabeth hesitated and bobbed her head too close to the microphone and then back again a bit too far. Finally, she offered a tentative, "Hello."

"Speak up," the announcer encouraged her, moving the microphone closer.

"Hello, I'm very excited to be here. Mr. Grant has been so wonderful." The crowd cheered, happy to be back on predictable ground. Photographic flashes put spots in her eyes. "Say, hello, Simon. This is my husband," she said dragging Simon to her side. "Say hello, Simon."

Simon frowned and leaned down to the microphone. "Good evening." His deep voice and crisp British accent caused a woman near them to wail and then swoon dramatically into her friend's arms.

"You should hear him say good morning," Elizabeth quipped.

The announcer muscled in front of them. "Thank you, I see Dick Powell and Joan Blondell have just arrived!"

Elizabeth started to step away from the mike, but leaned back in and quickly said, "May the force be with you."

Simon pulled her away to join Alan as the announcer frowned at her and started his brief commercial pitch. "Dew Deodorant. When nervousness makes you perspire, ladies, Dew will keep your secret."

Inside the theater they were greeted by more press and posed for a few more shots before Alan was led away to a special box at the back of the theater to sit with other stars and VIPs. They promised to meet by the south fountain in the forecourt after the movie was over. One of the dozens of usherettes who were dressed as chorus girls took Simon's and Elizabeth's tickets and led them out of the lobby and into the theater.

The interior was as outlandish and wonderful as the outside. Towering, broad columns lined the edges of the theater and reached up to a ceiling that was covered with racing dragons and detailed inlay like a crazy Chinese restaurant. Crushed red velvet seats and enormous red curtains topped the entire bilious design.

They were seated along the aisle and the buzz of anticipation made the room surge with electricity. A pair of tall gentlemen asked to slip past them and into two seats in the middle of the row. Elizabeth stood and tried not to gape as a very young Henry Fonda and Jimmy Stewart made their way past.

When the lights dimmed and the crowd settled, the orchestra started a lively rendition of a song Elizabeth didn't recognize, but the crowd certainly did and broke out in spontaneous and raucous applause. A single spotlight lit center stage and a chorus girl danced her way into it. And then another, and another until the stage was filled with dancing girls. The crowd loved it. The girls did two numbers of synchronized, Rockettes-style dancing before a little man with frizzy white hair introduced the film.

As the lights dimmed and the Mammoth Studio's mascot trumpeted, it was easy to forget what tonight really was and what the future held. Elizabeth slipped her hand into Simon's. Whatever it was, they'd face it together.

CHAPTER SEVENTEEN

JUST AS THE CREDITS began to roll, an usher in the traditional organ grinder monkey costume, came down the aisle and leaned down to ask, "Mr. and Mrs. Cross?"

"Yes?" Simon said.

"Mr. Grant wants to see you. If you'll follow me?"

With the theater still in darkness they followed the usher up the aisle and through the nearly empty lobby. He led them down a long hall to what looked like a series of back offices.

"Is everything all right?" Elizabeth asked.

"Fine, ma'am," the usher said as he stopped at a door nearly at the end of the hall. "He asked that you wait in here for him."

Simon felt it at the same moment she did. Something was wrong. He stopped and took hold of Elizabeth's elbow. She didn't need the hard squeeze to know he was on edge.

"I think we'd like to use the restroom first," Simon said. "They're back this way?" he said casually taking a step backward and subtly moving Elizabeth behind him.

The usher's smile slid off his face as he reached into the waistband of his uniform and pulled out a gun.

For a moment, Elizabeth idly wondered if she and Simon could get some sort of time travel kidnapping insurance policy.

The man jerked his head to the side toward the door. "Get in."

Simon didn't move and she could see him calculating the odds of successfully disarming the other man. The usher must have seen something in Simon's face because he grinned and took a step back. "I wouldn't."

He waved the muzzle of the gun toward the door again. "Move."

They had no choice now. Simon reached back and took Elizabeth's hand. He held on tight as he opened the door and they stepped in.

They'd barely set foot inside the door when someone grabbed Elizabeth from behind. A hand clamped over her mouth and she screamed into the cloth he was holding. She heard Simon try to call her name and the brief sounds of a struggle. She smelled the slightly sweet cloying odor and knew what would come next. Everything started to fade. Like the end of an old silent film, her conscious world shrank into a small circle of light as darkness overtook it and finally snuffed it out.

When she came to, she had the same sharp headache she'd had the last time someone had chloroformed her. Hazily, Elizabeth realized it was probably not good that she had a previous experience to compare this one to. She blinked a few times to try to clear her head and felt someone gently slapping her cheek.

She groaned and tried to shove the hand away, but her arms felt like they weighed a hundred pounds. "Stop it," she mumbled and leaned her head back.

Finally, the world started to focus and she saw a hand holding out a glass of water. "Drink this."

Her mouth was dry and pasty. She forced her arms to answer her command to move, but realized her wrists were bound together. She cradled the glass between her hands and forced a few sips down. The gauzy film that had coated her eyes finally washed away and she looked up to see where she was and who had given her water.

Benny Roth smiled and took the glass from her hand before she thought to throw it at him. It looked like they were in one of Benny's clubs, but it was closed and empty and only a few dim lights lit the room. Benny set the glass down on the table he was leaning against. Behind him, sitting at the table was Mr. Thorn, looking bored.

"Where's Simon?" Elizabeth tried to stand when strong hands clamped on her shoulder from behind and shoved her back down.

Benny took a revolver from his jacket pocket, making sure she saw it, before placing it on the table next to him. He nodded to his left and she followed his gaze.

"Simon!" she called out. He was tied to a chair about ten feet away; his head slumped forward onto his chest, his arms tied behind his back. She tried to stand again and the same hands shoved her back down.

"He put up a pretty good fight," Benny said, motioning to someone behind her. "Took two of mine to take him down."

He glared with displeasure at the big man who'd moved to Simon. "Wake him up."

The man grabbed Simon's hair. Elizabeth winced and struggled to stay in her seat as the man roughly pulled Simon's head up. She could see the blood tricking down Simon's chin and staining the white collar of his shirt. She wasn't tied to the chair like Simon was, but with her hands bound, all she could manage if she did stand would be an awkward two-handed Captain Kirk chop and somehow she doubted that would do anything to the gorilla manhandling Simon.

The big man slapped Simon on the side of the face a few times until he was roused enough that he could hold his head up on his own. The man picked up a glass of water but instead of offering it to Simon he threw it in his face. Simon coughed, choking on some of the water. Elizabeth clenched her hands into fists in frustration. Simon shook his head and blinked his eyes. She saw it in his eyes—the moment he realized what had happened. He struggled against his bindings and called out for her.

"I'm here," she said. "I'm okay."

The panic in his eyes dulled to a cold anger as he looked at her and then at Roth. He tried to speak, but his throat was dry. He coughed again and glared at Roth. "What do you want?"

"Direct," Roth said. "I like that." He shrugged. "I'm a business man. This is a negotiation."

Roth stood and wagged a finger in the air. "You two've been snoopin' around. Even sent a man around to my clubs." He put a hand over his heart. "My place of business. I take that sort of thing kinda personal. But, I coulda overlooked it, until you stuck your nose in with my brother."

Elizabeth remembered what Simon had said about Walter and Benny on the night of the attempt on Sam Roth's life and the pieces fell together in her mind. "You put Walter up to it."

"Kid was a sap. I shoulda just used one of my own. Cops woulda looked the other way for a price. Now, he's just another mess I had to clean up." He sucked air between his teeth and tapped his temple. "Stupid kid. Didn't use his brain. Tried to sing. My boys on the inside made sure it was a short song."

Elizabeth glanced over at Simon. They both knew what that meant. That poor boy.

"But," Benny said, "like I said, I'm a business man and I've got more pressing matters." He looked at his man and jerked his head. "Get out."

The big man nodded and left them alone in the empty club.

"Let her go," Simon said.

Benny laughed. "These noble types, they're such a pain in the ass." He walked over to Simon and gently, almost playfully, slapped him on the cheek. "Like I said, I'm here for business." He stood next to Simon's chair. "I'm offering you a deal."

"What's that?" Simon asked.

"Not you," Benny said. "Her."

Elizabeth caught Simon's eye before she looked up to Benny. "Not interested."

"I think you will be. You see, you got something I need and I got something you want." He put his hand on Simon's shoulder.

Elizabeth's heart started to sink.

"No doubt, you nosed around enough with Grant to know about my little deal with Thorn. So, I don't have to explain the particulars." Benny shrugged. "Sufficed to say, you're gonna offer your soul in exchange for mine," Benny said as he lifted the gun to Simon's temple. "Or I'm gonna blow your husband's brains out."

Elizabeth was sure her heart had stopped beating, just stopped. Her mouth went dry and her eyes shifted from the barrel of the gun pressed against Simon's head to his eyes, eyes that were pleading with her.

"No," Simon said.

Benny pushed the gun harder against Simon's head. "Shut up."

Simon's eyes silently begged her to not to do it, everything about him was imploring her not to do this for him, not to do this to him.

But, of course, she would. She had to.

Maybe it was all just a trick of Thorn's. Another manipulation. They didn't know for certain that souls even existed much less that Thorn could somehow take control of one. She would agree. Of course, she would agree. And, even if Thorn was the Devil himself, Simon's life meant more to her than anything in the world, even her own soul. She could tell by the pained look in his eyes that Simon knew that too.

Elizabeth turned to look at Thorn who was still sitting at one of the tables, but was looking far more interested than he had before. "I thought," Elizabeth said, her mind scrambling to find purchase on something, "that it wouldn't work this way. That…that the soul had to be offered freely. Coercion would void the contract."

Thorn flattened his palms on the table. "True," he said.

Elizabeth felt her heart start beating again.

"To an extent," he continued as he stood. "You'd be hard pressed to find a man or woman willing to give their soul up for eternity if they weren't under some sort of duress."

"Being under duress and being coerced are not the same," Simon said.

"Perhaps the causes are not," Thorn said, "but the results are."

"That's not fair," Elizabeth said, knowing it was a stupid thing to say. There was nothing fair about any of this.

Thorn spread his arms, palms up. "You are, of course, free to say no to the offer."

Elizabeth glanced at Simon. That was no choice at all.

"There are different types of arrangements," Thorn said. "This is standard. Boilerplate stuff really. Sam Roth's arrangement is much more complex."

That got Benny's attention. "What do ya mean, his arrangement?"

Thorn smiled, a big fat fake *oh dear, did I let that slip* smile. He was toying with Benny like a cat with a mouse. "He… introduces me to people. Prospects."

"What do ya mean, he…" Elizabeth saw the penny drop. "Like me? He sold me out to you?"

"And Grant and the girl and countless others."

"That son of a bitch," Benny said. "My own brother."

Benny somehow managed to ignore the fact that he'd just tried to murder Sam. And would have if they hadn't saved his life, she realized with a sinking feeling.

"Ours is a long-term arrangement," Thorn said. "Yours, however, is not. And the proverbial clock is ticking, Mr. Roth."

Benny pushed up his sleeve and looked at his watch. "All right, let's get on with it." He waved the gun at Simon.

"What happens," Elizabeth asked, "after?"

"Elizabeth," Simon ground out.

Thorn ignored Simon and leaned back against the table in front of Elizabeth. "Your soul takes the place of Mr. Roth's and he's free to go about his normal life."

"And me?"

"Well," Thorn said, lacing his fingers and resting them against his thigh, "most die rather quickly."

"Elizabeth," Simon said, struggling against his bonds, "you can't do this."

Benny cocked his gun. "What's it gonna be?"

"Just a signature on a simple contract," Thorn said, pulling a large folded paper from his inner jacket pocket.

"Elizabeth!"

"Hurry up!" Benny yelled.

"All right," Elizabeth said. "I'll do it."

"No," Simon's voice was so filled with despair that she didn't dare look at him.

"I have your word that Simon will be unharmed?"

Thorn smiled. "You have my word."

Elizabeth stood and held up her bound hands. "I'll need these untied."

Benny barked out a laugh of triumph and came over to untie her wrists. Elizabeth looked past him. Simon was straining against the ropes that held him to the chair. His face was so anguished that it took Elizabeth's breath away.

Benny grabbed her arm and turned her back toward him and Thorn. Thorn took a pen from his pocket and gave it to Benny, who held it out for her. Elizabeth gripped the pen and looked at it. Could someone really give his or her soul away with such a simple thing?

She turned to Simon and said, "I'm sorry." When she turned back, she twisted the pen into her palm to grip it and spun back around. Her fist clutched the pen and she aimed for Roth's neck. The nib dug deep into the side of his throat.

Benny's cry of pain was frozen by shock. His eyes flashed as he shoved her away and reached up to feel the pen sticking out of his neck. "You bitch." He raised his gun hand and Elizabeth closed her eyes. *I'll find you, Simon,* she thought and waited to die.

She heard the shot and then another. She flinched at the sound of each, but realized she hadn't been hit. But she didn't dare open her eyes. She couldn't bear to.

"Elizabeth?"

She let out a breath. Simon. Her legs wobbled beneath her in relief. She opened her eyes and turned to see Jack, gun drawn, walking up behind him. "You okay, kid?"

"Jack! Thank God. I'm fine." She rushed to Simon's side. "Are you all right?" Her eyes rapidly scanned him for any injury.

"For God's sake, untie me."

Her fingers fumbled with the knots, glancing once quickly over to see Roth lying in a heap on the floor, red stains blossoming against his white shirt.

Once she'd managed to release Simon from his bonds, he stood and pulled her into his arms. "What were you thinking?"

"We gotta go," Jack said as he stood over Benny Roth's body, gun trained on Thorn. "What about him?"

Elizabeth heard a commotion coming from the other room. Roth's men would be there soon. She looked quickly at Thorn.

He was as unfazed and as placid as ever. Devil or not, he was dangerous, but she couldn't murder anyone in cold blood. Not even him. "Leave him."

Jack looked like he might shoot Thorn anyway, but pointed them toward the back door where he'd snuck in. "Car's 'round back."

Jack hurried past Elizabeth as they made their way to the door. Elizabeth turned around just as they were at the exit and saw Thorn standing over Roth's body. Something drifted up in the air and Thorn caught it in his handkerchief. He folded it and put it into his pocket, turned to her and smiled.

CHAPTER EIGHTEEN

ELIZABETH REALLY NEEDED TO practice running in high heels. Women in the movies always made it look so effortless. It wasn't. There was effort. Lots of it. Between the shoes and the long hem of her dress, she probably would have taken several headers if Simon hadn't been at her side.

"Here," Jack said as he skidded to a stop on the sidewalk next to a sporty looking convertible.

"Where'd you get this?" Elizabeth asked. Jack definitely hadn't had this car when they'd arrived.

Simon struggled with opening the passenger side door for her and she shoved his hands away to try for herself. A gunshot pinged off a lamppost just a few feet away from them. Simon bent down and swept Elizabeth off her feet. He dropped her into the front seat and then leapt into the back. "Get this thing going!"

Jack, who'd gotten behind the wheel, grumbled and shoved his head further under the dash. "I'm trying!" Another shot took out the tail light just as the car roared to life. He threw it in gear and the tires squealed as they sped off into the night.

"Everybody okay?" Jack said once they'd gotten a few blocks away and it was clear they weren't being followed.

"Fine," Elizabeth said catching her breath.

"Where did you learn how to do that?" Simon asked her, reaching for his own neck.

"Godfather Two," she said. "Or was it Three? I think it was Three."

Simon just shook his head in response.

"How did you find us?" Elizabeth asked Jack.

He looked over at her briefly. "I got worried. Tonight's the big night and when you didn't call…I phoned Alan Grant's place—"

In the panic of the last few minutes she'd nearly forgotten about him. "Is he all right?"

"He was pretty well on his way to getting plastered," Jack said. "But he was plenty worried about you. When you didn't show up after the movie…" Jack shook his head and let the rest of the thought fall away.

"How did you know where we were?" Simon asked.

"I didn't, but I figured Roth had something to do with it. So, I went around to his clubs. After he saw me at dinner with you, his wheels were turning. I shoulda figured it sooner." He glanced at Elizabeth. "I'm sorry."

"You saved our bacon, again," Elizabeth said as she touched his shoulder. "I don't think you have anything to be sorry for."

"Yeah," Jack said, but he didn't sound convinced.

"It's already after eleven o'clock," Simon said, leaning forward. "We need to get to Grant's before midnight. Do you know where it is?"

Jack nodded. "We're gonna be cutting it close."

"Will we make it?"

"If we don't hit traffic."

They did.

The Los Angeles of the past wasn't nearly as congested as the Los Angeles of the future, but it didn't take much to create a traffic jam, even late at night. They had to take a short detour and lost precious time, even though Jack drove like a man in a stolen car—which they were. When they pulled into Grant's driveway, it was ten minutes to midnight.

"Grant?" Simon called out into the darkened foyer of the house.

Elizabeth pointed to light coming from the hall where Alan's study was. They rushed toward it, but Jack edged into the lead, his gun drawn. He pushed open the door.

Alan stood in front of his desk and turned around at the sound. "Who are—" he started until he saw Elizabeth step out from behind Jack. "Thank God. Are you all right?"

Elizabeth slipped into the room past Jack. "We're fine."

Alan quirked an eyebrow at that, as he saw the blood on Simon's collar.

"Mostly," Elizabeth added. "Benny Roth—"

"Was a fool," a voice said.

She knew who it was before she turned. Thorn sat casually in a reading chair on the far side of the room.

Jack stepped forward, gun leveled at Thorn. "How'd he get here before us?"

Thorn shrugged. "The traffic in this city is devilish, isn't it?"

Had he just taken another route? Had he somehow caused the accident that delayed them? Everything about Thorn made Elizabeth's head spin. And he knew it and enjoyed every moment of discomfort.

"That," Thorn said, nodding toward Jack's gun, "won't solve your problem."

Jack took two steps forward. "One way to find out."

Elizabeth wasn't sure if Jack would have actually pulled the trigger or not, but she couldn't let him. "Don't."

Jack turned questioningly to Simon who glared at Thorn, but eventually shook his head. Jack looked back to Thorn. "I don't like people who hurt my friends. You do anything else to hurt them, anything," Jack said, "and I will kill you."

"I would expect nothing else," Thorn said not threatened in the least. In fact, Thorn lingered over Jack, his dark eyes taking measure. He must have liked what he found. He smiled and said, "We should talk later. I can help you with your...problem."

Jack took a step forward and only Elizabeth's hand on his arm stopped him.

Thorn ignored the little display and checked his watch as he stood. "Well, it's just about time. That is, unless, someone here would like to make an offer."

"No," Simon and Alan said in unison.

Thorn smiled and shrugged.

"There has to be something we can do," Elizabeth said.

The grandfather clock in the corner ticked loudly in the silence of the room, seeming to grow louder and louder with every passing second.

"Perhaps doing nothing is the answer," Simon said. "Roth, Ruby, they both died because they panicked. They were ultimately responsible for their own deaths."

Alan shook his head. "There have been others. I suppose you could explain them away as well, but the coincidence is simply too much. I don't know how he does it," he said looking at Thorn, "but I believe *he* does."

If Alan really felt that way, if he believed, true or not, it would be a self-fulfilling prophecy. Elizabeth could tell from the look in Simon's eyes that he'd come to the same conclusion. "There has to be something," she said.

"It's been a good run," Alan said.

"Don't talk like that."

Alan took Elizabeth's hand. "Would you...?" Alan asked her. "Make sure my affairs are in order. Perhaps I can do some of the good then that I failed to do before."

He didn't need to say her name, didn't dare say her name, but Elizabeth knew he was talking about Grace. "It won't come to that."

"Oh, Lucia." Alan kissed her hand and his pale blue eyes glistened in the dim light.

The clock's pendulum swung back and forth, each swing a step closer to the end. Elizabeth couldn't stand the feeling of being so helpless. There had to be something she could do. She turned to Thorn. "Please? Release him."

"Just because you ask so nicely?" Thorn said scornfully. "No, I don't think so. We made a bargain and it's time he paid the price."

"You tricked him. It's not fair."

"He chose his path." Thorn seemed to get a little taller, a little broader and a lot scarier. "And now it's come to an end."

"Wait," Simon said, stepping forward. "The contract. We want to see the contract."

"As I said before." Thorn's patience was starting to wear thin. "Only the parties to the contract may ask to see it."

"Damn it, man," Simon bellowed at Alan. "Ask to see it!"

Alan sighed. "What good can it do now?"

Elizabeth grabbed Alan's arms. "Don't give up. You have something wonderful to live for. Fight!"

Alan smiled ruefully, but he nodded. "May I see the contract?" he said, clearly thinking it was a useless exercise.

Thorn frowned, but pulled the large folded papers from his jacket pocket and held them out. "You have five minutes."

Simon snatched the papers from his hand and unfolded them. He read the first page quickly and then the second. And then he read them again.

"Anything?" Elizabeth asked coming to his side.

Simon handed her the page and started to pace the length of the room. The clock ticked on.

Elizabeth read the contract, but she couldn't see any loophole. There was no way out. The minute hand inched closer to midnight.

Jack moved closer to Thorn, his gun ready and poised. Alan stood stock still, pulled between hope and despair.

Abruptly, Simon stopped pacing and ran a hand through his hair and rubbed the back of his neck. "Eternity," he said softly. "You said something about that earlier and it's been bothering me ever since," Simon said to Thorn.

He reached out to Elizabeth and she handed him back the contract. He read a passage aloud, "…and the soul will be consigned to the second party for all of eternity…Eternity."

Suddenly, Simon spun around toward Thorn. "You said these contracts were drawn to meet the standards of the laws of man."

Thorn nodded slowly.

Simon held out the contract as he strode toward him. "The laws of man govern this?"

"Yes."

Simon struggled to find the words. The clock ticked relentlessly behind him. He spun around and strode toward Alan. "That law book you were using before? Where is it?"

Alan shook his head. "I don't know."

"Yes!" Elizabeth said, running to the bookshelves. "I remember seeing it when we were in here last time. He was working on his will. It's here. I know it's here."

Anxiously, she skimmed the shelves. Simon came to her side and they hurriedly traced the spines along the shelves. "There's a rule...what is it called? Perpetuity! The Rule Against Perpetuities. Eternity. That's a violation. I knew there was something about that part of it. It's been eating away at me ever since he said it."

Thorn's face was impassive.

"It's common law," Simon said as he and Elizabeth frantically searched the shelves.

Thorn was not convinced. "I need more than your word, I'm afraid."

The clock on the wall kept ticking.

"Here!" Elizabeth cried as she pulled a heavy volume off the shelf and handed it to Simon.

Simon handed her the contract and flipped through the pages of *Black's Law Dictionary* so quickly they nearly tore. "You can't require a contract with a duration of eternity. It invalidates the contract," he said as he tried to find the right section.

"This!" he said triumphantly and then read, "Common-law rule prohibiting a grant of an estate unless the interest must vest, if at all, no later than 21 years (plus a period of gestation to cover a posthumous birth) after the death of some person alive when the interest was created."

Thorn shook his head. The grandfather clock began to chime. "That is estate law, property, valuables."

Elizabeth's heart raced well ahead of the clock. "You said it though. You said 'a man has nothing of more value than his soul.'"

The clock continued to chime.

Thorn's confidence slipped. "Yes."

Another chime. And another.

"You can't have a man's soul or anything else for eternity. This contract," Simon said with a hell of a lot more confidence then she felt. He took the contract from Elizabeth's hand and tossed it onto the desk and the papers fluttered down to the surface, "is void."

Thorn stared down at it and then looked first to Simon and then Elizabeth with eyes so flat and so chilling she literally felt her blood go cold. "It appears so," he said.

The clock struck its final chimes. Midnight. And then silence. The moment stretched out until Alan let out a breath.

"I'm free? Good heavens," Alan said then smiled his apology at Thorn. "Sorry, poor choice of words."

Thorn was not amused. He looked at Simon and inclined his head in a deferential nod. He picked up the contract and tore the papers in half before tossing them back onto the desk. "Very well played."

Thorn started toward the door. Jack stepped forward, his gun still out, but Elizabeth put a stilling hand on his arm.

Thorn stopped when he reached the doorway and turned back. "Until we meet again," he said in a way that would stay with both of them for years to come, "Mr. and Mrs. Cross."

Thorn glared at Simon in some sort of final challenge.

"Good bye, Mr. Thorn," Elizabeth said and then turned her back on him. Alan took Elizabeth's hand; his was shaking even more than hers. Simon pulled her to his side and when she turned back to the door Thorn was already gone.

Alan squeezed her hand and she turned back to him. She didn't know what to say and pulled him into a hug. His arms held her close and she could feel his racing heart.

"Well done," he said, "well done." Alan released her and shook Simon's hand. "How did you know?"

Elizabeth had wondered that herself. "Some estate thing in England?"

Simon blushed slightly and rubbed his chin. "I saw it in a movie."

CHAPTER NINETEEN

THE SMALL GROUP HADN'T wanted to leave each other, but fatigue finally won out. Jack drove Simon and Elizabeth back to their hotel with a promise to meet them at his apartment the following afternoon. They'd done what they'd set out to do—saved Alan Grant. It was time to go home.

They'd left Grant in Peter's care, shaken, but alive. He wasn't the only one, Simon thought as he toweled off from his shower. His tête-à-tête with Roth's men had left him bruised and sore, but it was the experience with Roth himself that had left him shaken.

Simon pulled on his pajama bottoms and tied them loosely. They hung low on his hips and he saw the beginnings of what would be an unsightly bruise just above his hipbone. Well, it could have been worse, he thought. Much, much worse.

He ran the towel over his chest once more, tossed it onto the bathroom counter and shut the light. Elizabeth was already in bed. Rolling up the far-too-long sleeves of their shared pajamas top, she sat propped up against the headrest. The smile on her face as she looked at him as he came into the room faded. Her eyes sought out the marks on his ribs and shoulder.

"Those look painful," she said.

"They are," Simon confessed as he turned off his bedside lamp and slid into bed with her.

Elizabeth frowned and eased the sheet down to his waist. She leaned over to examine his injuries. Her delicate touch along his skin made his breath catch.

"Did I hurt you?"

"No," Simon said, but he stilled her hands anyway. "The bruises will heal. But…" He let out a breath and looked at her hand so small in his. "Losing you? Never."

Despite the discomfort, he propped himself up on his elbow to face her. "You must promise me," he said, "never to do that again." He felt an echo of the surge of blind panic he'd felt when she'd agreed to give her soul for his life. "Never."

Elizabeth touched the edge of his jaw and shook her head. "You haven't cornered the market on loving someone, Simon."

"Elizabeth——"

"I would do it again. You mean everything to me too, you know."

He frowned at that. She leaned back into her pillow and turned her head to smile at him triumphantly, clearly thinking she'd put an end to it.

"If that's the case," he said sweeping her hair away from her neck so he could touch the bare skin, "then my wishes should preclude your own. And I want you alive."

She scrunched up her face in that adorable way she did when she was winding up and getting ready to unleash a wave of Elizabeth logic. "That's not fair."

"Isn't it?" Simon said. "You love me more than anything—"

"But you love me more than anything too," she parried. "Don't you?"

Simon chuckled and caressed her cheek. "You know I do." His hand drifted down her cheek and over her shoulder.

"Then it seems we've reached an impasse," she said firmly. "There's only one thing to do."

His hand continued down her body until it slipped under the sheet and hem of her shirt and came to rest on the curve of her hip. "And what's that?" he asked. His long fingers gently brushed along her soft skin and then sloped down to her small waist.

"What's what?" she said.

"The one thing we should do," Simon said, his hand lingering along the delicate skin at her side.

Her eyes fluttered and he loved the way they'd darkened when they focused on him again.

"Stay alive," she said, trying to arch into his touch.

He leaned in just about to kiss her, his hand urging her closer. He whispered in her ear as he pulled her against him. "A very, very good plan."

THE FOLLOWING MORNING THEY called the studio and gave their notice before heading over to Alan Grant's one last time. Peter stood out front loading suitcases into the limousine. They found Alan inside standing at the window in his study. It reminded Elizabeth of the way they'd found him just a few days ago, but then the room had been filled with despair. Now, there was nothing but hope.

"Going somewhere?" Simon asked.

Alan turned around and grinned. "Yes, as a matter of fact." He shook Simon's hand and kissed Elizabeth's cheek. "Considering the circumstances, Sam Roth has kindly agreed to let me out of my contract," Alan said with a small laugh before turning to look back out of the window. "And that monstrosity of a picture."

"I wish there was something we could do about him," Elizabeth said. Sam Roth had been complicit in everything Thorn had done here. She hated the idea that he was going to get away with it.

"We saw Peter out front," Simon said. "Going somewhere?"

"Taking a trip to Philadelphia. I have a new adventure waiting for me." Elizabeth followed his gaze. His eyes were glued to his daughter, Grace, who was in the backyard, squatting down and touching the water in the pool. "I just hope I'm good enough for the part," he added softly.

Grace shook the water off her hand and looked back to the house. She saw them in the window and waved.

Elizabeth waved back. "I think you're going to be a hit."

"Role of a lifetime," Alan said, his gaze lingering a moment longer on his daughter. He turned back to them. "And what of you? More souls to save?"

Simon and Elizabeth shared a look. "Something like that," Simon said.

Alan looked out of the window again and Grace waved to him, asking him to come outside. He nodded and then turned back. Alan held out his hand again to Simon. "Thank you." And then turned to Elizabeth. His pale blue eyes said everything he couldn't. She was going to miss this man. He took her hand. "Goodbye, my dear Lucia. Will I ever see you again?"

Elizabeth wanted to say yes. So much. "You never know."

He smiled sadly. "I shall never forget you. After all, how often does a man get to meet his very own guardian angel?"

With that he kissed her hand, and then walked away. They watched him through the window as he went down the steps and walked over to Grace. She held up something for his approval. A flower. He smiled and tucked it into the buttonhole in his lapel. Then, he slipped his arm over her shoulder and together they walked away, along the edge of the pool and into the start of a new life.

Jack knocked on Betty's door, stepped back and braced himself. Going behind enemy lines in France had been easier than this. Risking his life for his country had been easy. Risking his heart for it was much harder. He took a few deep breaths and waited. A few moments later, he heard the lock turn and the door opened.

"John? I thought you…" Betty smiled and shook her head, shooing away whatever thought had taken root and then pulled the door open for him to enter. "Come in."

Jack forced himself not to. "I can't."

She leaned against the edge of the door and cocked her head to the side. "What do you mean?"

He wanted to kiss her. He wanted to kiss just one last time. "I'm leaving."

She laughed, but it died quickly. "Leaving?"

It was hardly adequate, but all he had to offer her. "I'm sorry."

That was all it took—those two little words. He could see her shutting down inside. He could *see* it happen.

"Yeah?" she said, her voice betraying the hurt she felt.

He didn't know what to say. What could he possibly say? He'd tried to think of a way. He'd lain awake all night trying to think of some scenario that kept them together. But, try as he might there was no changing the fact that she couldn't leave and he couldn't stay. One more sacrifice.

"I've gotta leave town. I don't know when I'll be back."

"Weeks? Months?"

"Longer," he said. Forever. The look on her face made his stomach clench. "I should have just walked away—"

"Looks to me like that's what you're doing." Her pain was mixed with anger now. He deserved it all and more.

"I knew it was wrong from the start." He wanted so badly to come clean, to walk away from his knowing he'd finally been honest. But the truth wouldn't come. It couldn't. He was a man made of lies. It was who he was. It was who the world needed him to be. "I just hoped...I just wanted...."

"Oh, you got what you wanted alright," Betty said bitterly, but her eyes were filled with shame. He'd done that to her. "So, this was all some game to you. Some...fling? I'm surprised you even had the guts to come back."

Tears glistened in her eyes and Jack clenched his hands at his sides to keep from reaching out to her.

"I wanted to see you." His arms ached to hold her again.

As if she'd heard his thoughts, she held out her arms, but it was not an invitation. "Get a good look," she said, angrily.

"Betty—"

"Save it. Just..." She started to close the door in his face, but stopped. "You know, I should've known nothin' in this town was real. You're just another shadow."

She slammed the door in his face, but he barely heard it. The words "another shadow" hit him like a punch to the gut.

She'd said that before. She'd say that again. It all fell into place and Jack felt sick.

It was him. He was the man who'd betrayed Betty. The man who still haunted her in the future. The man who'd broken her heart. It was him.

Jack stood on her doorstep as it all sank in, as the truth of what he'd done kicked him in the face. Someone in Betty's past had kept them apart in 1938. The man who'd been just a shadow.

Jack barked out a quick, harsh laugh. He'd done it to himself. The other man he'd hated all those years was him. What a fool he was. What a sad, lonely fool.

Everything had played out just as it had before and would again, time and again. He would lose her in 1938, go to war, find Simon and Elizabeth, come back here and lose her again.

In a daze, he looked at her front door. He would give anything to change things. But he couldn't. Not now.

Not now, he thought as he slowly made his way down the path away from her home. Not now, but some day. Some day, he would find her again. He didn't know when or how. His past might be written, but his future was not.

Some day, he thought. Some day.

SIMON AND ELIZABETH WAITED in their hotel for Jack.

"We could still go to the studio," Elizabeth said.

Simon sighed heavily. They'd been over it before, but she couldn't let it go. "And do what? Accuse Sam Roth of introducing people?"

Elizabeth hated leaving him and Thorn unpunished. But, Simon was right, there was nothing they could do. "I know. Sometimes I wish we hadn't saved his hide at that party."

"You don't mean that."

Elizabeth wrinkled her nose. "No."

Simon rubbed her shoulder comfortingly and gave it a squeeze. "I know it's frustrating. We won't always be able to know exactly where everyone stands. All we can do is our best."

Just as she was really starting to get her umbrage on, he had to go and be all logical and reassuring.

"We came here to save Alan Grant," he continued. "And I'd say we did that rather well."

Elizabeth had to agree. Seeing Alan with his daughter had made it all worthwhile, even if they had made what could be a formidable enemy in Thorn.

One thing was bothering her though. "What movie did you see that in? The thing about the Rule Against Perpetuities?"

Simon cleared his throat and, was that a blush? "*Body Heat*," he said quickly and looked at the watch impatiently.

Elizabeth's smile could not have been any broader. "And you don't watch movies."

Simon fiddled needlessly with the watch. "Where is Wells?"

"He'll be here," Elizabeth assured him.

Right on cue, there was a knock at the door. Elizabeth opened it. Jack looked terrible. His eyes were red and the tension coming off him was palpable. "Are you all right?" she asked.

Jack set his jaw and nodded. "Let's just get the hell out of here."

Simon looked to Elizabeth for confirmation and then put the key into the watch. The electric blue light took them home.

A STRONG WIND BLEW open the French doors of Edgar Thorn's study. Papers on the desk in the empty room rustled in the breeze. Another gust came, stronger than before. Papers whipped up caught in the current and the glass from a large case on the wall behind the desk rattled until the latch worked itself loose.

The door to the case flew open with such force it crashed into the wall and shards of glass fell to the floor. Inside, the butterflies' wings started to quiver. A single pin fell to the floor hitting a shard of glass with a sharp tink. One large butterfly flew from the case. It started to fall to the floor, but its translucent wings caught in the wind and it rose up and began to fly. Another pin fell and then another, until they'd all rained down onto the floor mixing with glass.

Another butterfly flew from the case and then another and then another. The wind swirled inside the room and then slowly died. But the butterflies still flew. They dipped and rose in that awkward, beautiful way butterflies do and fluttered through the open doors and out into the world again, free.

THE END

NOTE TO READERS

THANK YOU FOR READING The Devil's Due; I truly hope you enjoyed reading it as much as I enjoyed writing it.

I know that was a cruel twist of fate Jack had to endure, but don't worry! I have a feeling he and Betty will find each other again some day. Life has a lot left in store for him, and, of course, for Simon and Elizabeth.

Thanks again for reading!

If you enjoyed this book, please consider posting a short review.

Leaving reviews for books you enjoy is a wonderful way to help spread the word and invaluable to authors.

Have an idea for a time and/or location you'd like to see Simon & Elizabeth (or Jack) visit? Drop me a line or come on by Facebook and let me know. I have quite a few ideas for future adventures, but would love to hear from you!

Sign up for the new releases newsletter!

moniquemartin.weebly.com

ALSO BY MONIQUE MARTIN

Out of Time: A Time Travel Mystery (Book #1, Out of Time)
When the Walls Fell (Book #2, Out of Time)
Fragments (Book #3, Out of Time)

ABOUT THE AUTHOR

MONIQUE WAS BORN IN Houston, Texas, but her family soon moved to Southern California. She grew up on both coasts, living in Connecticut and California. She currently resides in Southern California with her naughty Siamese cat, Monkey.

She's currently working on an adaptation of one of her screenplays, several short stories and novels and the next book in the Out of Time series.

For news and information about Monique and upcoming releases, please visit:

http://moniquemartin.weebly.com/